A FANTASY SHARED

A Husband's Darkest Fantasy
Becomes a Brutal Reality

Leah Jenkins

CONTENTS

THE IDEA

T he house, once bursting with the constant chatter of teenage arguments, the slamming of doors, and the pounding bass of music, now sat in a tranquil silence. The empty nest was supposed to feel hollow, a quiet reminder of time passing, but instead, it felt like the turning of a page—a strange, electrifying new beginning. At forty, I stood in front of the large bay window that overlooked the garden, the late afternoon sun casting long, golden shadows that danced across the living room floor. The silence pressed around me, warm and charged, an almost tangible entity that held secrets I hadn't even realized were there.

Our sex life had always been good, or so I had believed during those busy years when passion had to squeeze itself between soccer practices and work deadlines. But with the kids gone, there was room now—room to explore, to rediscover each other in a way that felt like venturing into uncharted territory. Steve, my husband of over two decades, wore his tailored suits like armor, his tie impeccably knotted as he commanded boardrooms with a voice that brooked no argument. He was the kind of man who, with a few words and a steely look, could make or break entire deals that steered the future of the company.

There had always been subtle hints, little things that, in hindsight, made perfect sense. The way his eyes lingered when I took control in the bedroom, or how he'd pause, expectant and almost nervous, when I made teasing remarks. But it all came to a head one night after a party. We'd both been drinking, the champagne bubbles mingling with the heady laughter and the freedom of the moment. By the time we stumbled into our bedroom, the air between us was thick with the lingering buzz of the evening. I slipped out of my dress, the silk whispering as it pooled at my feet, and turned to see Steve watching me with a look that made my breath catch.

A playful grin curved my lips. "Kneel," I joked, expecting a laugh or a smirk. But instead, a shadow passed over his expression, deeper and more vulnerable than I'd ever seen. Without a word, he sank to his knees, the motion deliberate and reverent. The world around us seemed to pause as he leaned forward, pressing his lips to my thigh before tracing a slow path upward.

The shock of it sent a jolt through me, replaced quickly by a rush of heat as his tongue found me. My fingers buried themselves in his hair, and I looked down, meeting his gaze. What I saw there made my pulse quicken—a plea, a silent question, and the raw honesty of a man who wanted this, needed this. It was as if a door had opened, revealing a secret part of him that had been waiting, hidden beneath layers of polished control.

The days that followed were different, the echoes of that night settling comfortably between us. The next time I leaned back on the bed with an arch of my eyebrow, he dropped to his knees without hesitation. The power I held in those moments, the way he surrendered without shame, became an addictive thrill. Demanding oral sex turned into a regular indulgence, and each time, the silent exchange of trust and desire bound us closer. Steve, who ruled the corporate world with an iron will, now found solace in surrendering to me, and I discovered in myself a boldness that felt like coming home.

The realization had been intoxicating. The air between us was no longer mundane; it crackled with a secret that bound us tighter than any vow ever could. Even now, as the sun dipped lower in the sky, casting the room in shades of amber, I felt the flutter of anticipation low in my belly. The boundaries we had always respected had suddenly become suggestions, daring us to push, to test, to discover just how far we were willing to go to satisfy that itch. The air was thick with unspoken questions, the kind that made my skin prickle and my heart beat faster. And in that breathless silence, I realized that everything I thought I knew about us was only the beginning.

The bedroom was bathed in the warm, muted glow of the bedside lamp, casting soft shadows that moved with us as the night unfurled. I ran my fingers down Steve's chest, feeling the steady beat of his heart beneath the taut skin, and smirked as I lowered myself between his thighs. The anticipation in his eyes sent a rush of heat through me, and I took my time, trailing kisses over the fine line of dark hair that led to his hardening cock. I glanced up, meeting his gaze, and the way he looked at me—part longing, part surrender—ignited a deeper hunger within me.

My tongue flicked out, tracing the tip of his cock, savoring the taste of his precum as his breath hitched. I wrapped my lips around him, taking him slow at first, teasing with gentle suction as my hand stroked the base with a steady rhythm. The soft groan that slipped from his lips was music to my ears, urging me to take him deeper, hollowing my cheeks as I did. The way he gasped my name, a desperate whisper, sent a pulse of satisfaction through me. I picked up the pace, feeling the tension coil in his body, drawing him closer to the edge.

Before he could reach that peak, I pulled away, wiping my mouth with a playful smirk as he looked down at me with wide, pleading eyes. "Not yet," I teased, crawling over him, my skin brushing against his until I straddled his chest. The shift in power was palpable, and it was a thrill to feel it, to see him staring up at me, waiting. Without hesitation, I shifted forward, pressing my pussy against his mouth, the warmth of his breath fanning over my slick folds as he took me in.

His tongue was eager, lapping at my clit with an abandon that left me gasping. Each flick, each slow circle, sent waves of pleasure rolling through me, making my thighs tremble. My fingers tangled in his hair, guiding him, urging him on as his hands gripped my hips, pulling me closer. I rocked against his face, eyes closing as the pleasure built, a delicious ache spreading through me. His moans were muffled, vibrating against my pussy, pushing me closer and closer until I had to bite down on my lip to stifle the cry that threatened to spill out.

When I couldn't hold back any longer, I shifted back, leaning down to kiss him, tasting myself on his lips before positioning myself over his cock. His eyes, glazed and dark with desire, met mine as I sank down, taking him in inch by inch. The sensation was electric, a shiver that started in my core and radiated outward. I moved slowly at first, savoring the feel of him stretching and filling me, the way his hands gripped my waist, fingertips pressing into my skin as if he couldn't get enough.

I began to ride him, rolling my hips in a rhythm that left us both breathless, our bodies moving together as if we were made for this. His eyes stayed locked on mine, filled with a mix of awe and need that made my pulse race. I leaned back, placing my hands on his chest for leverage, the change in angle making us both moan as the friction built to a fever pitch. The room was filled with the sound of our bodies meeting, the slap of skin against skin, the ragged breaths, and the whispered curses and names gasped into the warm air.

I felt the tension coiling tight in his body beneath me, the way his grip on my waist turned almost bruising as he held on. The pace quickened, our moans mingling in the heated space between us. I could see the way his eyes fluttered shut, the way his head pressed back into the pillows as he lost himself in the moment. His cock throbbed inside me, and I knew he was close.

"Cum for me, Steve," I whispered, leaning down until my breath grazed his ear. The command sent a shiver through him, his body responding instinctively. With a groan that came from deep in his chest, he bucked beneath me, the release hitting him hard as he spilled inside me. The heat of it, the sensation of him pulsing and emptying himself, sent my own pleasure spiraling, leaving me trembling and breathless.

For a moment, the room was filled only with the sounds of our ragged breathing, the echoes of our climax reverberating in the quiet. I collapsed onto his chest, feeling the rapid thump of his heart beneath my cheek, both of us slick with sweat and satisfaction. I traced lazy circles on his skin, a content smile playing on my lips. This was the intimacy I loved, the raw aftermath where everything felt connected and real.

But as the silence settled, the warmth between us shifted. I felt his body tense slightly beneath mine, a telltale sign that something was weighing on him. I propped myself up, searching his face for clues, but his eyes were fixed on the ceiling, lost in thought.

"Are you okay?" I asked, the question breaking through the heavy quiet. He blinked and turned to me, the flicker of uncertainty in his gaze making my stomach tighten.

"Yeah, I just…" His voice trailed off, and he sat up, pulling away from me enough that the cool air whispered against my skin. The way he rubbed the back of his neck—a nervous habit I hadn't seen in years—set my pulse racing with apprehension. "There's something I need to tell you," he said, his tone low and hesitant.

I shifted, drawing the sheet up around me as I watched him with wide eyes. "What is it?" The question hung between us, heavy and fragile, as if it might shatter under the weight of his response.

He took a deep breath, eyes darting to mine before shifting away again. "I've been holding onto this for a long time," he said. The room seemed to shrink, the air thickening with tension. "It's a fantasy… one I've never told you about."

My heart thudded faster, my mind racing ahead to fill in the blanks. Dressing up? Role-play? Something to add a little spice? I forced a small smile, trying to ease the tension. "Steve, whatever it is, you can tell me."

But he didn't smile. Instead, he looked at me with a mixture of desperation and fear, as if he were about to leap off a cliff and had no idea if he'd land safely. "I want to watch you with another man," he said finally, his voice cracking. "A black man. I want to watch him fuck you while I'm there… helping."

The words landed like a physical blow, knocking the air from my lungs. I stared at him, unable to process what I'd just heard. Steve, the confident, controlled man I thought I knew, had just revealed something that left me reeling. My pulse pounded in my ears, drowning out everything else as his confession sank in.

"What?" I whispered, my voice barely audible. The disbelief was thick, and the anger quickly followed, hot and overwhelming. "Are you serious? You want to see me with someone else? You want to see me used like that?"

The look on his face was one of utter devastation, but it only fueled my own. Years of shared intimacy and trust suddenly felt like they'd been upended. "I can't believe you," I said, pushing myself off the bed and grabbing my robe. The fury burned through me, the betrayal stinging in ways I didn't know were possible.

"Wait," he called, but the door slammed behind me before I could hear anything else.

The days that followed were a blur of cold silence. We didn't speak; we didn't even look at each other. Meals were eaten alone, conversations were nonexistent, and the chasm between us widened with each passing hour. I replayed his confession over and over, each time feeling that hot flush of anger and betrayal. How could he? How could the man I had built a life with want something so twisted, so completely unlike anything I thought we shared?

But beneath the anger, something else lingered—a question I wasn't ready to face. And as the days stretched into a week, the silence between us became unbearable, a testament to everything that had been laid bare.

The days after our argument were a storm of conflicting emotions. I moved through the house in a daze, haunted by Steve's confession, replaying the words in my mind until they lost their meaning, leaving only raw, jagged feelings in their place. Anger simmered beneath the surface, but something else did too —a gnawing sense of doubt that kept me from pushing it away completely. How could he want something like that? And how had I never noticed the longing hidden behind his composed exterior?

At night, I would lie awake, staring at the ceiling, wondering if this fantasy was a betrayal or just a buried desire that had festered in the dark corners of his mind. The more I thought about it, the more I realized that fantasies didn't have to be reality. They were safe spaces, untouchable places where the rules of life didn't apply. Maybe it was harmless, I told myself. Maybe it was something we could use, a way to stoke the embers that had started burning when we discovered his submissive side.

The idea took root, tentative and uncertain at first, but it grew. And soon, I found myself scrolling through online catalogs, cheeks flushing with a mix of excitement and embarrassment as I clicked on the item that made my heart race: a large, realistic black dildo. The thought of buying it in person was unthinkable; I could barely type in my card details without my hands shaking. When the discreet package arrived, I half-expected the mailman to give me a knowing look, but he handed it over with the same practiced disinterest as always.

That night, anticipation crackled in the air as I prepared myself. I slipped into a set of black lingerie, a lacy bra that lifted my breasts and crotchless panties that left me exposed and tingling. I looked at myself in the mirror, nerves fluttering in my stomach like a swarm of butterflies. This wasn't just for him—it was for me too. A way to reclaim control, to test the boundaries of our trust.

When Steve came home, I greeted him with a smile that hinted at mischief. He raised an eyebrow, curiosity lighting his eyes. "I have a surprise for you," I said, my voice steady despite the rush of adrenaline coursing through me. "Strip and get on the bed." His eyes widened, but he obeyed, shedding his clothes and lying back, watching me with that look of anticipation that always made my pulse race.

I stepped into the room, hips swaying, and his eyes roamed over my body, drinking in every inch of exposed skin. From the dresser, I pulled out the dildo, the sheer size of it making my heart thump as I held it up. His eyes darkened, breath catching as he realized what I had in my hands.

"Look at this," I said, my voice low and teasing. "I might not ever take another man inside me, but tonight, we're going to explore that little fantasy of yours." He swallowed hard, eyes glued to me as I ran the length of the toy over my chest, letting it glide between my breasts. The cool, smooth surface sent a shiver across my skin, and I caught his gaze, noting the way it was fixed on me with rapt attention.

I brought the head of the dildo to my lips, brushing it lightly before pressing a kiss to it, letting my tongue flick out to taste it. "Oh, your cock is so big," I said, my voice dripping with mock surprise, eyes locked with his as I took it into my mouth, inch by inch. Steve's breath grew ragged, and I could see the tension in his body as he watched me suck the rubber cock, my lips stretched around it, saliva glistening as I pulled back and licked up the shaft.

"Do you like that?" I whispered, my tone challenging. His nod was almost frantic, a soft moan escaping him as he watched. Encouraged, I slid my hand down my body, fingers brushing my clit, teasing myself as I continued to play with the dildo. "Too big for my pussy," I said with a mock whimper, pressing the head against my entrance, teasing him—and myself—with the slow push.

"Please! Not in my pussy," I said, voice trembling with exaggerated fear, eyes meeting his for a brief second before they fluttered closed. I could hear him shifting on the bed, his breathing uneven as I worked the toy inside me, inch by inch. The stretch was intoxicating, and I let out a moan, deep and genuine, that filled the room. "Oh, fuck me with that big black cock," I whispered, the words sparking something primal in him. He groaned, hand reaching out to touch himself, and I smiled, taking in his reaction.

I moved the dildo slowly, deliberately, feeling every ridge as I pulled it out and pushed it back in, hips bucking as the pleasure built. "So big," I panted, eyes locked on his as I repeated the words, watching the way his jaw clenched, his eyes blazing with a mix of lust and awe. "It feels so good."

The room was filled with the slick sounds of my arousal, my moans growing louder, more desperate as I rode the toy, my body trembling with the force of my impending climax. "Look at me, Steve," I gasped, the command sending a jolt through him. "Watch me cum on this big cock." His eyes never left mine, and as the wave of pleasure finally crested, I cried out, my body shuddering with the intensity of it. "So big," I whispered one last time, sinking down on the bed, breathless and sated.

The moment Steve's voice broke through the heady silence of the room, I realized how deeply my performance had affected him. His eyes were wild, his breath coming in shallow gasps, and I followed his gaze to see his cock, hard and straining, a bead of precum glistening at the tip. The sight sent a shiver of satisfaction through me. The power I wielded, the way he was undone by what he had just witnessed, made my heart pound with a heady mix of control and desire.

I crawled over to him, deliberately slow, letting my breasts brush against his chest, feeling the heat radiating from his skin. My lips hovered just above his, my breath mingling with his as I whispered, "Did you enjoy watching me suck that big black cock?" His eyes widened, a deep flush creeping up his neck, and he nodded, a strangled noise escaping his throat.

"Say it," I teased, my hand wrapping around the base of his cock, squeezing just enough to make him shudder.

"I loved it," he gasped, hips jerking forward, desperate for more.

I smiled, letting my tongue flick out to taste the precum pooling at the tip, salty and slick. His entire body tensed beneath me, muscles coiling as I traced the head with slow, deliberate licks. I savored the way he responded, the way his hands fisted in the sheets, fighting the urge to grab me. I wrapped my lips around him, taking him in inch by inch, hollowing my cheeks as I began to move, each slow bob of my head drawing a deep groan from him.

The tension in the room crackled, building as I kept my pace torturously slow, letting my tongue glide along the underside of his cock, tasting him, teasing him. His breath grew ragged, and I glanced up to see his face contorted with pleasure, eyes squeezed shut. The sight sent a pulse of heat through me, urging me on as I quickened my pace, letting my lips slide down to meet my hand, which stroked him with a matching rhythm.

Before I could register the change, he let out a strangled scream, hips bucking wildly as he came, hot and sudden. His hand shot out, fingers tangling in my hair as he tried to hold me in place, but I pulled back instantly, his cum splashing across my lips and chin. The taste hit me, bitter and slick, and I recoiled, wiping my mouth with the back of my hand as anger flared.

"God, I fucking hate cum," I spat, storming to the bathroom to wash the taste from my mouth. There it was: the one thing that could ruin even the most electrifying moment. There's something about it—the bitterness, the warmth, the way it clings to your tongue and slides down your throat—that makes my skin crawl. It didn't matter how many times I tried to get used to it; the second that taste hit my mouth, all I wanted was to wash it out, to scrub away the reminder of it. I'd rather do just about anything else than swallow. Spit or pull away, it didn't matter—I just *couldn't* stand it.

I turned the faucet on full blast, scrubbing at my lips until the bitterness was gone, glaring at my reflection as if it had betrayed me. The raw confession rang in my ears, echoing back, and I couldn't help but let out a small, frustrated laugh at the absurdity of the situation.

When I came back to bed, Steve was lying there, still catching his breath, eyes full of something between shame and satisfaction. I slipped into the sheets next to him, the silence stretching between us for a beat before I broke it. "You must have really enjoyed that," I said with a teasing lilt, smirking as his eyes darted away, embarrassment flickering across his face.

He opened his mouth to respond, but before he could, I felt the press of his lips trailing down my neck, a gentle kiss that sent a shiver skittering down my spine. He moved lower, the heat of his mouth tracing the curve of my breasts, leaving a wet path that tightened my nipples into hard peaks. I gasped as his tongue circled one, pulling it into his mouth before continuing down, his kisses turning wetter, needier.

When he reached my pussy, his eyes flicked up to meet mine, and I knew what was coming. My breath hitched as his tongue slid over my clit, slow and deliberate. He spread my legs wider, his hands pressing into my thighs to keep me open as he worked, each flick and swirl sending jolts of pleasure shooting through me. I arched my back, fingers gripping the sheets as his tongue found a rhythm, moving from soft licks to deep, needy plunges that made me cry out.

He knew exactly how to push me to the edge, the way his tongue alternated between teasing my clit and plunging into my soaked pussy. The slick sounds of his mouth on me, combined with the guttural moans that escaped him, pushed me higher, the pressure coiling tight in my core until it snapped, a wave of heat crashing over me as I came, hard and shuddering. My cries echoed in the room, thighs quivering as he held me through the aftershocks, lapping up every drop as if he were starving.

As I came down, chest heaving, I felt him shift, the press of his body against mine. I glanced down, eyes widening in surprise at the sight of his cock, rock hard and pressing against my thigh. My mouth parted in disbelief. He had never gotten hard again so quickly, never without at least an hour's rest, even on his best days.

Before I could voice my shock, he was on top of me, the head of his cock pressing against my entrance. I gasped as he pushed inside, the sudden stretch making me arch into him, nails digging into his back. The bed creaked beneath us as he set a frantic pace, driving into me with a force that made my tits bounce with each thrust. The room filled with the sound of our bodies meeting, the slick slap and ragged moans weaving together in a symphony of raw, primal need.

His hands gripped my hips, pulling me to meet each deep,

pounding thrust. My breath came in short, broken gasps, the sensation overwhelming as he pushed me close to the edge again. But before I could tip over, I felt him shudder, a guttural groan tearing from his throat as he came, his cock throbbing deep inside me. He collapsed beside me, chest heaving, the heat of his release still spreading through me as I lay there, unsatisfied but too stunned to move.

I sat up, feeling the warmth trickle down my thighs, irritation pricking at me as I realized I hadn't come again. But I couldn't deny that something had changed, something fundamental and unspoken that lingered between us. I went to clean up, wiping away the mess before sliding back into bed. Neither of us spoke, but in the quiet that followed, an unspoken understanding settled over us like a heavy, shared secret.

PUSHING THE BOUNDARIES

After that night, when the unspoken understanding settled between us, something changed. It was subtle at first—a lingering look, a touch that felt more deliberate—but the shift was there. I could feel it every time we were together, an edge that hadn't existed before. It wasn't long before Steve's need for those fantasies seeped into our daily life. The tension between us built, coiling tighter with each passing day, until it found its way into our bedroom in the most explicit ways.

One night, I decided to push the boundary a little further. We were lying in bed, the room dimly lit, casting warm shadows across his bare chest. I straddled him, my fingers curling around his cock, stroking him with slow, measured movements. His eyes locked onto mine, wide and dark with anticipation.

"Tell me how it would feel," I whispered, leaning down so my breath ghosted over his lips. "Tell me how you'd feel if I were getting fucked by a cock that made yours look small. A big, thick, black cock stretching me so deep I'd be moaning for him." The words were crude, raw, and I saw how they hit him. His eyes glazed over, a flush climbing up his neck, and his breathing turned ragged.

His hips thrust into my hand, desperate and needy. "Fuck, yes," he choked out, the sound strangled as if he were barely holding himself together. I tightened my grip, teasing him further, describing every sordid detail, how I'd gasp as I took that cock, how my pussy would strain around it. His moans grew louder, his body tense beneath me as he pushed closer to the edge.

When he came, it was violent, his body jerking as his cum spurted in thick ropes, hitting his chest and neck. The sight made my own core tighten, the power of watching him unravel so completely under my words.

The fantasies became more than just words over time; they seeped into the way he touched me, the way he worshipped me. One evening, he pulled me down onto the bed and spread my thighs apart, diving between them with a hunger that made me gasp. His tongue flicked over my clit, slow and torturous, as if savoring every taste. I gripped the sheets, biting back a moan as I looked down at him, his eyes closed, lost in the act.

"Do you know what I was thinking about today?" I teased, running my fingers through his hair, tugging just enough to get his attention. His eyes opened, hazy with lust, and he moaned against me, the vibration making my hips buck. "I was thinking about how it would feel to have a cock so big it would leave me ruined. One that would fill my mouth until my lips ached."

His response was immediate. His hands gripped my thighs tighter, and his tongue worked more fervently, as if he was trying to claim me back with every lick. "I bet you'd watch me struggle, wouldn't you, Steve? Watch me gag on it, my eyes watering as I tried to take him deeper," I continued, my own words sending a thrill through me. He groaned, a muffled sound that pushed me over the edge, my body trembling as I came hard against his mouth. He didn't stop, didn't come up for air until I was gasping, my legs quivering with the aftershocks.

And then there was that weekend away—a getaway meant to be relaxing, but one that turned into something much more intense. We made love slowly that night, the hotel sheets soft beneath me as Steve pushed into me with a deliberate pace, his eyes locked on mine. It felt different, deeper somehow, as if he was trying to reach some part of me that had always been just out of reach. My nails scratched lightly down his back as he thrust harder, making me cry out as he buried himself to the hilt.

"God, yes," I moaned, rolling my hips up to meet him, the rhythm between us perfect. The heat built, burning between us until his jaw clenched, his pace faltered, and he came, spilling deep inside me with a guttural moan. I caught my breath, looking down at the slick evidence of his release. And then a thought, wild and reckless, escaped my lips before I could stop it.

"What would you do," I said, meeting his eyes, "if that wasn't yours? If another man had just cum in me, and he was so big that there was no way you could ever make me cum after?"

The room went silent except for our labored breathing. His eyes widened, the flush that had begun to fade rushed back, and for a moment, he looked like he might deny it. But instead, he swallowed hard, and his voice, strained and low, said, "I'd... I'd clean you up." The confession was barely a whisper, but it hung between us, heavy and undeniable.

Embarrassment flooded his features, and he turned his head away, but I cupped his cheek, forcing him to meet my gaze. There was no mistaking the look in his eyes—desire, shame, and something else that mirrored the ache beginning to stir inside me. We lay there, both silent, but I knew that whatever line we had crossed was one we could never come back from. And part of me, the part that craved this dark, thrilling unknown, didn't want to.

At first, when Steve's fantasies began to edge into new territory, I felt a flicker of fear deep in my gut. The thought crossed my mind more than once: *Was he secretly gay?* It seemed like the only explanation at first, given the nature of his desires and the way he spoke about being involved with another man's cock. But as I did my own quiet research and stumbled upon the world of cuckold fetishes, the truth became clearer. This wasn't about attraction to men; it was about submission, power dynamics, and the thrill of vulnerability. Understanding that eased my initial panic and opened a door to curiosity that I never expected.

I started small, adding tiny touches to our stories, testing how he'd react when I pushed the boundaries. One evening, as we lay together, my voice soft and teasing, I told him how he might be "forced" to prepare my lover, sucking him off to get him ready for me. His reaction was instant and intense, his body stiffening beneath me, eyes widening as the words took root. The blush that spread across his cheeks wasn't embarrassment; it was raw desire. He looked at me, lips parted, breath shallow, as if waiting for more.

"Would you, Steve?" I whispered, trailing my fingers down his chest, feeling the rapid thump of his heart. "Would you get him ready for me, on your knees, taking him into your mouth?" He moaned, a sound so deep and needy that it sent a jolt through me. I realized then how deeply this ran for him, how much he craved this fantasy of submission and humiliation.

It was a dance, careful and deliberate. I kept my tone serious, my expressions thoughtful. The one thing I knew not to do—the advice my mother had given me years ago—was to never laugh at a man's fantasy. "Men's egos," she'd said with a knowing look, "are fragile things. If they trust you with their desires, handle it with care, no matter what it is." So I took that advice to heart, no matter how strange or taboo the ideas became.

When Steve began hinting at being humiliated by my imaginary black "bull," I didn't flinch. He spoke in fragments, embarrassed at first, afraid of my reaction. "Would you… would you laugh at me if I said…?" he'd start, voice trailing off, eyes averted.

"No," I'd reply firmly, turning his face back to mine so he could see the sincerity in my expression. "I would never laugh at you." The relief that washed over him in those moments was palpable, making the connection between us even stronger. I would weave stories where he watched, powerless and eager, as I took another man—tales that left him trembling by the end, body slick with sweat and need.

Sometimes, in the quiet moments after, when his breathing evened out and the room settled into a peaceful silence, he'd turn to me, eyes searching. "Would you really do it? Would you really let him fuck you like that?" The question always hung between us, heavy and bittersweet. I knew he wanted me to say yes, that the thought of it fed some deep, dark place inside him. But reality was different. I'd trace my fingers over his arm, offering a small, sad smile.

"No, Steve. I'm yours. You're the only man I'll ever be with," I'd say softly. The disappointment that flickered across his face was hard to ignore, but it was always fleeting. He'd nod, accepting it, and pull me closer, content to keep the line between fantasy and reality intact. He didn't push, never asked more than I was willing to give. Instead, he reveled in the fantasy, in the stories I spun that made him come harder than he ever had before.

It wasn't always easy for me, navigating this new terrain. There were moments when I questioned what it said about us, about our marriage. But the more we explored, the more I realized that it was about trust, about letting him show me the most vulnerable parts of himself and holding that trust like a precious, fragile thing. It wasn't about losing control; it was about finding a new kind of intimacy, one that was raw, unguarded, and deeply binding.

And as I watched him, eyes glazed and body shaking after another whispered story of submission, I knew that we had ventured into something deeper than just fantasy. It was the place where he could be stripped of all his power, laid bare, and still feel loved. It was a discovery, not just of him, but of us, and the connection that grew from it was unlike anything I'd known.

As Steve's forty-first birthday approached, I could sense a shift in his mood. He'd been quieter, introspective, the lines around his eyes deeper, and the usual spark that lit up his face was dimmed. I tried to lift his spirits with little gestures—his favorite meals, a new watch, plans for a weekend getaway—but nothing seemed to snap him out of the funk. The thought of how to make this birthday special gnawed at me. What could I possibly get him when he already had everything money could buy?

The answer, of course, lay in the deepest corners of his desires, ones I'd carefully navigated over the past months. I knew that if anything could ignite that spark, it would be seeing me engage with another man. The idea of going all the way was still unthinkable—I valued our marriage too much and the idea of crossing that line felt like a betrayal. But what if there was a middle ground? Something that was wicked enough to indulge his fantasies but not so far that it felt like infidelity.

A blowjob felt too intimate, too close to cheating. But a handjob? It was daring, yes, but in my mind, it skirted the edge of fidelity without crossing into it. Still, the question lingered: *Would that be enough for him?*

I mulled it over, glass of wine in hand, as the plan started to form in my mind. If this was truly about his need to be humiliated, to be the "cuckold" he spoke of, then maybe I could make it even more tantalizing by adding layers of teasing and control. The idea excited and terrified me in equal measure, but the thought of making his fantasies come to life and seeing the raw desire in his eyes pushed me forward.

The next hurdle was finding the right person. I knew I couldn't involve anyone from our community—it would be disastrous if word got out. And though Steve would probably jump at the chance to help me set this up, I wanted to surprise him, to show him that I was willing to step into this dark, unexplored space for him.

I sat down with my laptop, heart pounding, and logged into a swingers website Steve had casually mentioned months ago, one he used to browse when the kids were out of the house and we were still dipping our toes into shared fantasies. The site was more sophisticated than I'd expected, filled with profiles that ranged from tasteful to explicit. I sipped my wine, scrolling through potential matches, my pulse quickening at the idea of what I was about to do.

I read profile after profile, looking for someone who matched my criteria: respectful, experienced, and willing to abide by strict limits. Some of the messages I received were immediate turn-offs —men who clearly hadn't read my profile or who pushed for more than I was willing to give. A few promising ones turned out to be unavailable or disinterested once I explained that full sex was off the table. One joker even left the contact information for a pizza place, which earned him an immediate block.

Just as I was about to give up, my phone buzzed with a notification. It was a response from a man named Christian, whose profile I had messaged earlier. He was tall, broad-shouldered, with a confident smile and eyes that held a mischievous glint. His profile spoke of discretion, experience, and respect for boundaries—exactly what I needed. My heart thudded as I opened the message.

"Hi, I got your note. I'm interested and willing to meet your conditions. When would you like to talk more about this?"

I set my wine glass down, fingers trembling slightly as I typed back. The reality of what I was doing hit me in waves, excitement mixing with nerves as I arranged a time to talk. Christian's deep voice came through clearly when we spoke the next evening, warm and direct. He was polite, patient as I explained my intentions and limits, and asked thoughtful questions that reassured me he was exactly who he said he was.

The plan started to solidify, each detail falling into place as the date approached. I could already picture Steve's reaction, the shock, the lust, the hunger that would spark in his eyes when he realized what I had arranged. The thought of that moment made my skin tingle, anticipation curling in my stomach as I imagined his response when he found out just how far I was willing to go for him.

My conversation with Christian, whom I now knew by his online handle "ChristianBlackUK," had moved to a private chat on the swingers website, where we could exchange messages securely. The screen glowed softly in the dim light of my living room as I sat, glass of wine in hand, heart thudding in my chest.

Christian: Thanks for reaching out. I can definitely work within your limits, and discretion is a given. I know how sensitive these things can be.

His messages were always polite, direct, and tinged with a confidence that calmed my nerves. As we continued our back-and-forth, he sent me a few photos to reassure me of his trustworthiness—first, a picture of him dressed casually, leaning against a car with a confident smirk. The next was a shirtless photo, his chest broad and well-defined, dark skin glistening under the sun. I felt a flush creep up my neck as I took in the sight, my imagination wandering before I snapped myself back to the task at hand.

Me: Thank you for the pictures. It helps to see who I'm talking to. You're comfortable with everything we talked about? The boundaries are important.

There was a pause before the next message, and I bit my lip, waiting.

Christian: Completely. This is about making the fantasy real but safe. I get that. Here's one more pic for you—it's soft, so don't worry. The surprise is part of the fun.

The notification pinged, and my eyes widened as I opened the new image. His cock, soft but undeniably large even in its relaxed state, rested against his thigh. The reality of what I was arranging hit me like a jolt, but there was no mistaking the curiosity and heat that simmered beneath my nervousness. I swallowed hard, feeling a rush of excitement mingled with doubt.

Me: I appreciate the photos. I see what you mean by surprise, haha.

I typed the message quickly, my fingers trembling slightly. I had to remind myself this was all for Steve, for the glimmer of excitement and happiness I hoped to see in his eyes.

Christian: Trust me, the hard version is better saved for later. Keeps it interesting. Are you feeling okay about this?

The question, so straightforward, brought the bubbling conflict back to the forefront of my mind. Was I really okay with this? The logical part of me screamed caution, reminding me that this was more than just whispered fantasies and shared stories. This was real, tangible, and about to cross the threshold between imagination and reality. But the emotional part, the side that loved Steve enough to walk this razor-thin line, whispered encouragement.

Me: Nervous, but excited. This is new for both of us, and I want it to go well.

Christian: It will. Just remember, this is as much about you as it is about him. You need to be comfortable, too.

I leaned back in my chair, eyes lingering on the photos and the string of messages that marked the beginning of something significant. I took a long sip of my wine, letting the warmth settle in my chest. The reality of what I was planning left my body humming with adrenaline and doubt, and as I stared at the screen, I couldn't help but wonder if this would truly be the gift that broke through Steve's lingering melancholy or if it would lead us into territory we weren't prepared to navigate.

Later that evening, as the plan solidified, I approached Steve in the living room. He was slumped on the couch, eyes fixed on the TV, but his mind clearly elsewhere. I stepped behind him, wrapping my arms around his shoulders and pressing a kiss to his temple.

"I have a surprise for you on Friday," I murmured, my voice light but teasing enough to catch his attention. His eyes lit up, curiosity sparking to life as he looked up at me, a hint of the old smile playing on his lips.

"A surprise?" he echoed, the word laced with hope.

"Yes, but you have to be home early," I added. "No meetings, no excuses."

He chuckled softly, reaching up to touch my hand. "You drive a hard bargain. But I'll be here."

As I pulled back, I felt the weight of what I'd set in motion pressing down on me, a mix of nerves and anticipation that thrummed beneath my skin. Friday couldn't come soon enough, and with it, the answer to whether this gamble would bring us closer or push us apart.

THE POINT OF NO RETURN

The day had finally arrived. I stood in front of the mirror, adjusting the straps of my black push-up bra that pushed my breasts up and together, creating a cleavage that was impossible to ignore. The sheer silk blouse I wore clung to my curves, offering tantalizing glimpses of skin beneath. My short black leather skirt hugged my hips, barely covering the roundness of my ass. Stockings, held up by a garter belt, completed the outfit, along with the tiniest pair of sheer lace panties I dared to buy. The final touch was my black high heels, the ones that made my legs look longer, leaner. The reflection in the mirror stared back at me with a mix of defiance and nervous anticipation. I looked the part: sexy, confident, a little dangerous.

My heart thudded in my chest as I applied the last stroke of red lipstick, a color bold enough to match the occasion. Just as I capped the tube, I heard the front door creak open and Steve's familiar footsteps echo down the hall. He appeared in the doorway, his eyes widening as he took me in. The reaction was immediate—his gaze darkened, pupils dilating, and I noticed the unmistakable bulge forming in his pants. The surge of power that coursed through me was intoxicating.

"Do you think I look sexy?" I asked, my voice soft and teasing as I sauntered over to him. He nodded, words momentarily lost, his eyes roving hungrily over my body. I reached out, palming the hard length pressing against his trousers, and smirked. "Too bad this isn't for you," I whispered, giving him a final squeeze before stepping back. The confusion on his face was almost comical, a mixture of shock and desire. He opened his mouth as if to say something but thought better of it, turning on his heel and walking away, leaving me to my racing thoughts and the anticipation curling in my belly.

Moments later, the doorbell rang, and a shiver of excitement and nerves ran down my spine. I took a deep breath, smoothing my skirt before opening the door. There stood Christian—tall, broad-shouldered, with smooth, dark skin that gleamed under the porch light. His bald head and easy smile exuded confidence, but it was the glint in his eyes and the way he carried himself that hinted at the dominance I sensed from our conversations.

"Christian, this is my husband, Steve. Steve, meet Christian," I said, my voice steady despite the butterflies in my stomach. Steve's eyes widened as he processed what was happening, glancing between us as the weight of the situation sank in. I stepped closer to Steve, leaning in so only he could hear. "If you're a very good boy and do everything I say, you'll get to watch me jerk him off when we get back," I whispered. His eyes went dark with desire, and I saw his cock throb visibly through the fabric of his pants. The tension in the room crackled, unspoken understandings exchanged in glances.

I hadn't expected Christian to be so attractive, and that realization added a new layer to my nerves. Growing up, I hadn't given much attention to black men—it was just the way I was raised—but seeing him up close, with his imposing frame and confident smile, stirred something deep inside me. A guilty, thrilling excitement twisted in my chest as I took his arm, feeling the hard muscle beneath his shirt.

"But first," I said, breaking the silence, "Christian's had a long trip, and I thought we'd go out for dinner." The three of us made our way outside, and I felt an unexpected thrill walking beside Christian as Steve walked ahead to get the car ready. My heart beat faster, a cheap, guilty kind of thrill bubbling under my skin at the thought of neighbors catching a glimpse of us together.

When Steve pulled up, I slid into the back seat with Christian, leaving Steve to drive. The space between Christian and me was electric, the scent of his cologne mixing with the leather of the car seats. The moment the car began to move, Christian draped his arm over my shoulders, casual and possessive. Steve's eyes darted to the rear-view mirror, trying to maintain his composure, but I could see the way his knuckles tightened on the steering wheel.

"You have a sexy wife, Steve," Christian said, his deep voice breaking the silence. There was a hint of challenge in his tone, the kind that made my pulse quicken. Steve's eyes flickered to me, then back to the road.

"I agree," Steve managed, his voice strained, the tension in the car thick enough to cut.

Christian's hand shifted, fingers trailing lightly down my arm. "Has she ever been with a black man before?" he asked, his gaze meeting mine. The question was directed at me, but I felt Steve's reaction like a tangible pulse in the air.

"No," I said softly, glancing at Steve in the mirror before turning to Christian. "But my husband is more than willing to let me try." The words rolled off my tongue, bold and teasing, and I felt Steve's breath catch even from where I sat.

Christian's grin widened. "Mmm, a sexy girl like you has never gone black? Well, we need to correct that," he said, leaning in and pressing his lips to mine. The kiss was firm, confident, and left me breathless. My nipples hardened instantly, pressing against the thin fabric of my blouse as my head spun with the rush of sensation. Steve's reaction was immediate; the car swerved slightly before he regained control, his face flushed with a mix of shock and desire.

I broke the kiss, a nervous giggle escaping me as I glanced at Steve. "Careful, or we'll stop," I warned, my voice breathy. Christian leaned back with a smirk, glancing out the window as if nothing had happened. At the next red light, his hand found its way to my thigh, squeezing just enough to make me gasp. The heat flared between my legs, and I placed my hand over his, gently guiding it away. Not yet, I thought, the anticipation building in my chest like a coiled spring.

We chose a diner at the edge of town, a place where the chance of seeing someone we knew was slim to none. The neon sign cast a faint, flickering glow across the parking lot as we stepped inside, the warm, greasy scent of comfort food enveloping us. Christian and I slid into one side of the booth, the leather seat sticking slightly to my thighs, while Steve sat across from us, eyes darting nervously around the room as if on high alert. It was a quiet declaration of the shift in power, an unspoken acknowledgment that this night was different.

I noticed the subtle looks we drew from the other patrons, eyes glancing over Christian and me with varying reactions—curiosity, shock, judgment, even envy. The realization sent a rush through me, an unexpected sense of power that made my skin tingle. The subtle rebellion of sitting beside Christian, leaning into the dynamic we had constructed, felt bold, even thrilling. I was acutely aware of every movement, every brush of his arm against mine, every look Steve sent across the table, eyes catching on the way Christian's hand rested possessively on the back of the booth.

The conversation at dinner was light, punctuated by Christian's rich, confident laughter that put me at ease even as my nerves simmered beneath the surface. Steve watched us with a mixture of fascination and discomfort, his hands gripping his utensils a bit too tightly. My eyes met his now and then, offering a silent reassurance that was as much for me as it was for him.

After dinner, as the cool night air wrapped around us, I decided to push the teasing further. "Let's go downtown," I said, a sly smile playing on my lips. "Christian knows a club we should check out." Steve's eyes flickered with apprehension, but he nodded, ever the willing participant. The drive was filled with the low hum of the radio and the sound of my heartbeat thrumming in my ears as I felt Christian's presence beside me, solid and imposing.

The club was alive with thumping bass and flashing lights, the crowd moving in a blur of color and motion. Christian led me onto the dance floor, leaving Steve at a table near the edge with a drink in hand. The music was infectious, and I felt the beat pulse through my body as I started to move. Christian's hands hovered near my waist, close enough to feel his warmth but not quite touching. It was a silent promise, a tease that left my skin buzzing.

I let go of my reservations, rolling my hips and arching my back, feeling the fabric of my skirt ride up slightly with each movement. Christian matched my energy, his eyes locked on mine with a smoldering intensity. When he finally stepped closer, the space between us disappeared, and I felt him—hard and thick, pressing against my thigh as we moved together. The realization hit me like a jolt, my breath catching in my throat. The heat that surged through me was immediate and undeniable. I shifted my body, pressing back into him just enough to feel the outline of his cock more clearly.

A mix of emotions flooded me: excitement, guilt, curiosity, and a rush of power that left me breathless. The feeling of him— solid, almost impossibly large—sent a shiver through me, and I wondered fleetingly what it would feel like if this were more than just a tease. The thought made my cheeks flush, and I bit my lip to stifle a moan as Christian's hand brushed against the small of my back, guiding me closer.

The air between us was charged, and every nerve in my body felt alive, hyper-aware of the way Steve's eyes were glued to us from across the room. His expression was a mixture of longing and disbelief, and I could almost see the war waging inside him—the thrill of seeing his fantasy come to life colliding with the reality of watching me in another man's arms.

A slow song came on, and Christian pulled me even closer, his hands finally settling on my hips. I moved against him, the hard line of his cock pressing into my thigh more firmly now. It felt almost surreal, the heat pooling between my legs as I leaned my head back against his chest, letting the rhythm guide us. His breath was warm against my ear, and he let out a low, approving hum that made my skin tingle.

"You're driving him crazy, you know that?" Christian whispered, his voice a deep, smooth rumble that sent a shiver down my spine. I glanced at Steve, whose eyes were wide, mouth slightly parted as he took in the scene, his chest rising and falling with rapid breaths. The sight of him, so caught between desire and torment, pushed me further.

The moment became even more intense when another man approached, nodding at Christian with a silent request to cut in. Christian's eyes met mine, and he smirked before stepping back, giving me a nod as if to say, *Go ahead.* The man's hands found my waist, and I glanced at Steve as I moved with my new partner, his eyes following every touch, every sway of my hips.

I found out later just how pivotal that conversation was, the one that unfolded while I danced in the embrace of another man. Christian returned to the table, his movements confident and smooth, like a predator circling its prey. He leaned over the table, close enough for Steve to catch the subtle scent of his cologne, earthy and musky. Steve's eyes were trained on me, watching as I laughed and moved to the beat, oblivious to the tension brewing at the edge of the dance floor.

"That's one hot lady you've got there," Christian began, his voice low but carrying over the thrum of the music. The comment jolted Steve out of his reverie, and he turned his gaze to Christian, eyes narrowed, jaw clenched.

"Yeah," Steve said, his voice tight. He took a sip of his drink, the condensation from the glass slipping down his fingers. "I know."

Christian's eyes glinted with a challenge as he leaned in, elbows on the table, creating an intimacy that Steve couldn't ignore. "Are you sure you're ready for her to try Black?" he asked, his words deliberate, each one dropped like a stone into still water, sending ripples through the air. "You know what they say."

Steve's fingers tightened around his glass until his knuckles turned white. He hesitated, the silence stretching long enough for the music to shift to another song, the thumping bass rattling the table. He swallowed hard, eyes flicking back to where I was still dancing, my body pressed against my partner, hips swaying in time with the music.

"I'm pretty sure she's not going to go all the way," Steve finally replied, but there was a crack in his voice, a thread of doubt that Christian seized on immediately. A smirk played at the edges of Christian's lips as he tilted his head, watching Steve like a hawk.

"That's what she says now," Christian said, leaning back and crossing his arms over his broad chest. "But look at her." He nodded toward the dance floor, where I was moving with abandon, the heat between me and my partner palpable even from across the room. My eyes closed, a soft, almost private smile on my lips as I leaned into the music. "You see the way she's dancing, man? The way she's letting herself go? Trust me, in a few months, if you're not careful, she'll be begging for every Black cock she can find."

The words landed like a blow, and Steve's expression tightened, a mix of jealousy, fear, and undeniable arousal warring on his face. His pulse raced, and he felt his throat go dry as he tried to formulate a response. Christian's gaze was unwavering, unrelenting, as if he were peeling back the layers of Steve's carefully constructed fantasies to expose the raw truth beneath.

"You don't know her like I do," Steve said, the defensiveness in his tone obvious. He wanted to sound confident, certain, but even he could hear the uncertainty lacing his words.

Christian raised an eyebrow, a knowing look crossing his features. "Maybe. Or maybe she's just waiting for the right push," he said with a shrug, as if it were the most natural thing in the world. His eyes shifted back to me, taking in the way I laughed and tossed my hair back, my skin glowing under the club's neon lights. "Sometimes, all it takes is the right man."

Steve's jaw clenched so tightly that a muscle in his cheek jumped. He looked back at me, watching the way my new dance partner whispered something in my ear that made me giggle, my body leaning into him just a fraction more. The sight stirred a sick twist of jealousy in Steve's gut, but beneath that, buried so deep he almost didn't want to acknowledge it, was a pulse of arousal that made him shift uncomfortably in his seat.

Christian leaned forward again, his voice dropping so only Steve could hear. "This is more than just a fantasy now, isn't it? You need to be sure, or you'll end up watching her go further than you ever imagined."

Steve's breath came faster, each word cutting into him like a blade. The reality of what he had set in motion was staring him in the face, and for the first time, he wasn't sure if he was ready for it. He looked at Christian, saw the way the man's eyes gleamed with a mixture of challenge and amusement, and felt a chill run down his spine.

"I can handle it," Steve said, the words sounding hollow even to himself.

Christian chuckled, a low, rumbling sound that sent a shiver through the air. "We'll see," he said, leaning back in his chair, his attention drifting back to me as if to emphasize his point. The unspoken challenge hung between them, heavy and charged, as Steve watched me on the dance floor, caught between the fear of losing control and the thrill of giving in.

REALITY HITS

The ride home from the club was thick with silence, a current of tension running under the quiet that none of us dared to break. Steve kept his eyes on the road, the faint glow of the dashboard lights reflecting off his taut expression. Christian sat beside me in the back seat, his thigh pressed against mine, a silent reminder of what was about to happen. I stared out the window, the city lights blurring past, my heart thundering in my chest as I tried to steady my breathing.

When we pulled into the driveway, the familiar sight of our house, usually a place of comfort and routine, felt charged with an electricity I hadn't felt in years. This was it. The point of no return. My legs felt like jelly as I stepped out of the car, the cool night air doing nothing to calm the heat coursing through my body. I glanced at Steve, whose eyes flickered with a mix of apprehension and desire, and then at Christian, who met my gaze with a knowing smile, the promise of what was to come reflected in his dark eyes.

Inside, the living room felt smaller than usual, the air heavy as if the walls were holding their breath. I poured us all drinks, the clinking of ice in the glasses loud against the quiet. We sipped in silence, the alcohol burning a path down my throat, its warmth spreading through me and loosening the tight coil of nerves in my stomach. Christian's arm draped over the back of the couch, casual but commanding, and I sat close, feeling the heat radiating from him.

Steve settled into the armchair across from us, his posture stiff, the drink in his hand trembling just slightly. His eyes flicked between us, taking in the way Christian's hand rested on my shoulder, the subtle way I leaned into him. The room crackled with unspoken anticipation, each second stretching into an eternity as we waited for someone to make the first move.

Christian set his glass down on the table, the sound making me jump slightly. He turned to me, his eyes locking onto mine, searching, challenging. Without a word, he leaned in and kissed me. His lips were firm, confident, and the taste of whiskey and heat mingled as I kissed him back, my pulse pounding in my ears. The awareness that Steve was watching, eyes fixed on every movement, sent a thrill down my spine, sharp and undeniable.

When the kiss broke, I glanced at Steve. His chest rose and fell in quick, shallow breaths, his eyes wide and dark with a mixture of disbelief and arousal. This was it—the moment where fantasy met reality, where the whispered desires that had lived in the safety of our bedroom were now laid bare in the living room, raw and real.

Christian's hand slid down my arm, his fingers warm as they intertwined with mine. He guided my hand to his belt, and for a moment, the world seemed to tilt. It felt surreal, like I was outside of myself, watching this unfold from a distance. My fingers trembled as they brushed the cool metal of his belt buckle. The air between us was thick, each second measured in heartbeats.

I took a deep breath, my eyes darting to Steve one last time, searching for any sign of hesitation, any reason to stop. But his gaze was locked on my hand, his expression a cocktail of want, fear, and something deeper, something I couldn't quite name. His knuckles were white around the glass, his lips parted as if to speak, but no words came.

Slowly, I unbuckled Christian's belt, the leather sliding through the loops with a soft, deliberate sound. The noise seemed to echo in the silence, magnified by the charged atmosphere. My pulse thrummed in my throat, a rapid staccato that made my vision blur for a moment. I couldn't help but think about the people in my life —the PTA mothers who'd gossip over coffee, my neighbors who waved as they watered their lawns, even my daughters, grown now but still the little girls in my mind. What would they think if they saw me now, poised on the precipice of something so unrecognizably daring?

The button of Christian's jeans came next, the snap sounding louder than it should have, my fingers moving with a will of their own as I unsnapped it. I could feel his eyes on me, the weight of his anticipation mingling with my own. I reached for the zipper, and time seemed to slow. Each tooth of the zipper released with a metallic click that reverberated in my ears, as if the universe itself was holding its breath.

My heart pounded harder with every inch, the room spinning around me as the fly opened fully, revealing the dark waistband of his briefs beneath. My mouth was dry, my head light, and I swallowed hard, trying to ground myself in the reality of the moment. This wasn't a whispered fantasy in the dark or a teasing game. This was real, tangible, and inches away from going further than I ever imagined.

Christian stood up, the shift in his weight making the couch creak, and slid his jeans down over his hips. My breath caught as the fabric pooled at his feet, exposing him in the dim light. My eyes traveled up, taking in the sight of him—broad, powerful, and undeniably aroused. The realization hit me like a shockwave. It had been decades since I had seen another man's body this close, and the suddenness of it stole the breath from my lungs.

The tension in the room was palpable, electric, and I felt the moment hang in the air like a held note, trembling on the brink of what came next.

I stood there, heart pounding so hard it drowned out all other sounds. The room seemed to shrink, trapping us in this forbidden moment. My hands shook as they hovered over Christian's waistband, torn between what I knew was right and the insatiable need clawing at me from within. The air felt charged, crackling with heat and the unspoken desires we were dancing around. My husband's ragged breathing from across the room only amplified the tension. He sat, unmoving, eyes wide with a mix of awe, betrayal, and unmistakable arousal.

I swallowed hard, feeling my pulse race as my fingers dipped into Christian's briefs. The smooth skin beneath met my fingertips, warm and electric. When I finally wrapped my hand around him and pulled him free, I nearly gasped at the sight. Even half-hard, he was formidable, his cock an imposing presence that made my stomach clench and heat flare low in my abdomen. It seemed twice as thick as my husband's, a fact that sent a wave of guilt and illicit thrill rushing through me.

I hesitated, just for a moment, taking in the way his cock twitched beneath my touch, already growing in appreciation. The room fell silent, except for the rough, uneven breaths of my husband. I turned my gaze to him, searching his face for any sign of hesitation, but all I found was a tortured hunger. The way he looked at me, the mother of his children, the woman he thought he knew—it was as if he was seeing a side of me for the first time, and he couldn't look away.

"Do you like this, honey?" My voice trembled, low and sultry, laced with the raw edge of shame and excitement. "Do you like watching your wife do this?"

A strangled "yes" tore from his throat, more desperate than I'd ever heard him. He moved as if to reach into his pants, his hand hovering just above the zipper.

"No," I said sharply, tightening my grip on Christian's cock as a warning. "If you touch yourself, I stop."

Christian chuckled, the deep, rich sound vibrating through me. "You've got him on a short leash," he murmured, his dark eyes glinting with amusement and something more dangerous. His cock hardened fully in my hands, thick and pulsing, making my mouth go dry. I brought my second hand up, sliding both palms along the length of him as he grew impossibly large.

My husband's eyes widened, a groan escaping as he shifted in his seat, unable to tear his gaze from the sight. The way he watched made my skin flush with heat, a forbidden thrill shooting through me. I felt the wetness pooling between my legs, and I clenched my thighs, trying to ignore the ache that throbbed in time with my racing pulse.

"God, your cock is huge," I whispered, unable to stop myself. The admission sent a shudder through me, and I glanced at my husband, catching the way his eyes fluttered shut, head tilting back as he let out a guttural moan. His arousal was painfully obvious, straining against the fabric of his pants, and it sent a surge of power coursing through me. I was in control, and the realization made me dizzy.

Christian smirked, one hand reaching up to tug gently at my blouse, fingers brushing the edge where the fabric met my skin. His touch left a trail of fire that threatened to consume me. "Imagine how it'd feel inside you," he said, voice rough and unapologetic.

The thought alone made my breath hitch, and I squeezed my eyes shut for a second, battling the urge that surged within me. "Stop," I whispered, though it sounded weak even to my own ears.

But he didn't push further, didn't move, just stood there letting me fight my own battle. His confidence was intoxicating, a sharp contrast to the turmoil I felt. I continued to stroke him, the slickness of his precum aiding my movements as I picked up speed. My husband's breath came in harsh pants now, each sound spurring me on, breaking down my resolve bit by bit.

"Shit," I muttered, unable to tear my eyes from Christian's cock as it pulsed in my grip, heavy and hot. My heart thudded in my chest, and I bit my lip, feeling the wetness seep through my panties. The temptation was unbearable, gnawing at the edges of my control. I looked up at Christian, meeting his gaze, which was intense, challenging.

"Admit it," he said softly, leaning down so his face was close to mine, his breath warm against my cheek. "You're dying to taste it."

I glanced over at my husband again, seeing the torment in his eyes, the longing, the unspoken permission. His silence spoke volumes. He wanted this as much as I did, even if neither of us could admit it.

"Just once," Christian's voice broke through the tension, deep and commanding. "I won't cum until you kiss it."

A shiver ran down my spine, my chest rising and falling with rapid breaths. I turned to my husband, searching for any hint of protest, but he surprised me. He nodded, almost imperceptibly, a silent surrender. The final barrier fell, and I knew there was no going back.

Slowly, I leaned forward, my lips parting as I neared Christian's cock. The scent of him, musky and male, filled my senses, making my pulse race faster. I hesitated for just a moment before pressing a wet, open-mouthed kiss to the head of his cock, the taste sharp and electric on my tongue. It bordered on a suck, my lips clinging to him for an agonizing second longer than I intended. A ragged groan ripped from my husband, and I felt the room spin, the power of my actions sending a thrill through me.

I pulled back just enough to catch my breath, lips slick from the kiss that had left both Christian and my husband teetering on the edge. My fingers never left Christian's cock, moving in a slow, teasing rhythm that kept him hard and straining under my touch. The heat radiating from him was almost searing, each pulse against my palm a reminder of the power I held in this moment. My husband's eyes followed every stroke, his expression a perfect blend of torment and rapture.

"God, it's so thick," I said, marveling at the way my fingers barely met around his girth. My voice was breathless, unguarded. "Look at how hard it is. Honey, have you ever seen anything like this?" My husband's throat worked as he swallowed, unable to form words, just a slight shake of his head as his gaze locked on the sight of my hands gliding up and down Christian's length.

Christian's smirk deepened as he watched me, then he shifted his attention to my husband, eyes narrowing with a hint of challenge. "Is it bigger than his?" he asked, the question cutting through the tension like a blade. He didn't look away, his dark eyes drilling into my husband's, daring him to react.

I hesitated for a heartbeat, the room holding its breath. Then I spoke, my voice steady, matter-of-fact, and utterly damning. "Oh God, yes," I said, fingers tightening around Christian's cock. "There's no fucking comparison." The words hung in the air, making my husband flinch visibly, a shadow of pain flickering across his features. But beneath that pain, there was desire—raw, undeniable, and consuming.

Christian's breath turned ragged, each exhale growing shorter as tension coiled tighter in his body. I felt the shudder move through him, and I knew he was on the brink. My own chest rose and fell rapidly, skin flushed and tingling with anticipation. I looked at him, then at my husband, whose wide eyes were locked on us, every muscle in his body straining with barely controlled need.

This moment wasn't just about giving in to desire; it was about claiming control, showing both men who truly held the power here.

A sly smile curled my lips as I reached for the buttons of my blouse, one by one releasing the fabric until it slipped off my shoulders and fell away. I felt the cool air dance over my heated skin, goosebumps rising even as the room's heat enveloped me. My bra followed, unfastened with practiced ease, and I let it fall, baring my breasts to Christian and my husband's unblinking gaze.

Christian's eyes darkened, his muscles flexing as if he were barely holding himself back. I could see the restraint, the way he deferred to my unspoken command. I shifted his cock in my hands, positioning the head so it pressed firmly into the soft curve of my breasts, right against my hardened nipple. The sensation sent a thrill through me, heightening the urgency that throbbed low in my belly.

"Cum for me," I whispered, the words laced with both a demand and a promise. My voice carried the authority of someone who knew exactly what she wanted—and exactly how to get it. "Cum all over me, Christian. I want you to cover my white tits."

He groaned, a deep, guttural sound that vibrated through the room, eyes closing briefly as if the weight of my words had been too much to bear. When he opened them again, they were glazed with need, his body surrendering to the inevitable.

I glanced at my husband, whose face was flushed, mouth slightly open as he drank in the sight before him. His breathing came in quick, uneven pants, and his eyes shone with a mixture of desperation and awe. He was enraptured, helplessly caught in the spectacle I commanded.

Christian's cock jerked in my hands, and then, with a powerful shudder, the first hot spurt erupted from him. It landed in a thick, white rope across my chest, the warmth searing my skin. The next wave followed, splattering across the curves of my breasts and trailing up to my neck. The sensation was overwhelming, each pulse a reminder of the control I wielded over him. I kept stroking him, coaxing out every last drop, watching as his expression twisted with pleasure, eyes clenched shut as he surrendered to me completely.

"Look at that, honey," I said, my voice low, teasing. "Look at how much he's giving me. Isn't it incredible?" I glanced over at my husband, who looked as if he were about to come undone, his hands gripping the chair as if it were the only thing tethering him to the ground.

The final spurts dripped down my fingers, sticky and warm, until Christian's groans softened into heavy, satisfied breaths. He leaned forward, barely able to stand as I milked the last tremor from him, watching his body shudder one final time before he slumped back, catching himself on the edge of the table.

I lifted my hands, spreading his cum across my chest in deliberate, slow movements, letting it glisten in the dim light. The room smelled of sex and heat, the air heavy with the weight of what we'd just done. I caught my husband's eyes again, his pupils blown wide with desire, watching as I rubbed the sticky mess over my skin, claiming it, claiming my power.

Christian's breaths evened out, and he bent to retrieve a damp towel, gently wiping himself clean. But I didn't move, leaving the cum drying on my skin as a reminder, a declaration. When he straightened, he caught my eye and smiled, leaning in to brush a kiss against my temple, a gesture that was both intimate and loaded with meaning.

"Goodnight," he murmured, his voice soft, a stark contrast to the rawness of moments before. He cast one last glance at my husband, then left, leaving the room silent except for the thundering of our hearts.

I stood there, exposed, marked, and more in control than ever before.

I tilted my head back, a satisfied smirk playing on my lips as I regarded my husband. His chest rose and fell rapidly, eyes wide with the wild gleam of someone barely holding on to sanity. "Well, what did you think?" I asked, letting my voice drip with mock innocence, knowing full well the torment I was inflicting. He swallowed hard, his body taut, every muscle straining with the need to take me right then and there.

"Hold off," I commanded, watching his pupils dilate further at the command. He obeyed, trembling hands reaching to strip off his clothes until he stood bare before me, vulnerability etched in every line of his body. I continued to rub Christian's cum into my skin, massaging the sticky remnants over my chest and neck with deliberate slowness, letting it glisten like a trophy.

"Go to the bedroom," I said, holding his gaze with mine. "Bring me the black dildo and the bag. And come back naked." The way he turned, stumbling slightly in his haste, sent a thrill of power through me. I settled onto the couch, the leather cool beneath my heated skin, anticipation coiling tighter with each passing second.

When he returned, eyes dark with both desperation and submission, I leaned back, arching my body to display the sheen still covering me. His eyes roamed hungrily over me, but I shook my head, enjoying the way he winced with frustration. "Not yet, honey. Your torment isn't over."

"So," I began, letting my voice turn conversational, "you liked watching me with Christian, didn't you?" He nodded, the movement jerky and unrestrained. "Well, here's the truth—it turned me on too. His cock... it was so much bigger than yours." I let the words sink in, watching the flicker of pain and helpless arousal in his expression. "Do you know this black dildo is almost the same size as Christian's cock? Almost, but not quite." I held out my hand, palm up, and he passed it to me, fingers brushing mine with a shiver.

"Would you like to see me put it between my tits?" I asked, sliding the toy between the soft, still-glazed curves of my chest, pressing them around the shaft to mimic what I had just done. His breathing grew harsher, and I could see the ache in his body as he strained toward me. "Or maybe you'd prefer to see my mouth stretched around it?" I brought the toy to my lips, kissing the rubber head before slowly sliding it between my lips. The stretch was delicious, my mouth filled to capacity as I moved on it, eyes locked on his. His cock twitched, standing rigid and almost purple with need, and I could see him biting back a moan.

I released the dildo with a wet pop, a glistening string of saliva connecting my lips to the shaft for a moment before breaking. I handed it to him, a silent command. "Lube it up," I said, voice firm, unyielding. He obeyed, hands shaking as he squeezed the bottle, slicking the length until it shone under the low light. I stood and slid down to the floor in front of the couch, my knees pressing into the plush carpet.

"Would you like to see me take it?" I asked, arching a brow. "Would you like to see Christian's cock inside me, stretching me, fucking me deep?" The words made him shiver, eyes wild with longing. "You know it's far bigger than yours, right? What if I get addicted to it? What if that's all I want from now on?" I watched the conflict twist his expression, the shame and excitement warring for dominance.

His hand shook as he pressed the toy to my entrance, and I let out a low moan as it slid inside, filling me, stretching me. My own body arched, the slickness making it easy, pleasurable, perfect. His eyes were fixed on the point where the dildo disappeared into me, his breathing ragged. I started to move, thrusting my hips forward, taking more of it inside with each motion.

"Oh yes, fuck me with that big black cock," I said, my voice throaty and raw. His eyes snapped up to mine, desperation turning to pleading. "Do you know I could still get pregnant?" I continued, the taunt sending a jolt of power through me. "What would the neighbors say? What would your family think, seeing me walking around with a big, fat belly because of Christian? Would that turn you on, seeing me so completely claimed by another man?"

"Yes," he whispered, his voice breaking. "Please, let me... let me fuck you." His voice was almost a sob, his restraint barely holding.

I smiled, drawing out the silence as I moved slower, feeling the toy press deep inside me. "Only if you do one thing first," I said, tilting my head to meet his gaze. "If you ever want to see this again, you'll clean me up." His eyes widened, a tremor running through him as he understood. "Lick my tits and neck clean. Now."

He hesitated, his face a mixture of longing, shame, and defiance. The command I had just given hung in the air, heavy with implications that neither of us could ignore. His eyes flicked to my chest, the cum glistening on my skin like an unspoken challenge. I could see the war raging within him, a clash between pride and desire, between who he thought he was and what he was willing to become for me.

"Come on," I whispered, voice soft but unyielding. "This is what you wanted, isn't it? This is what those stories were leading to." I leaned back slightly, offering myself to him, watching as the struggle etched deeper lines into his expression. His jaw clenched, and for a heartbeat, I thought he might refuse. But then his shoulders slumped, a visible surrender, and he lowered his head.

He started hesitantly, tongue barely touching my skin. The first tentative swipe picked up a thin trail of cum, and I felt him shudder as the taste hit him. His throat bobbed, eyes squeezed shut as if trying to will himself through the moment. The gag was almost imperceptible, a quick jerk that made him pause. I let out a low, taunting laugh, threading my fingers through his hair, pressing him back down.

"That's it," I coaxed, voice dripping with power. "Lick it all up like a good boy."

He took a deep breath, the muscles in his jaw working as he pushed past the revulsion. His tongue flattened against my chest, licking a thick stripe through the mess, the warmth of his mouth sending a shiver across my skin. He traced the curve of my breast, gathering up the thick, cooling fluid, lips closing around my hardened nipple as he sucked it clean. The sight was intoxicating, the submissive act turning my arousal into a sharp, dizzying spike.

His eyes opened then, dark and resigned, as he continued his task. He moved with more confidence now, sliding his tongue across my other breast, catching a large blob of cum at the tip and swallowing it down with a strained groan. I felt the tension in his body, the way he trembled with both shame and arousal, the war within him now visible in the taut lines of his muscles.

"Good boy," I murmured as he worked his way up to my neck, each lick deliberate, thorough. His breath was warm, ragged against my skin, and I could feel the fight slipping from him with every pass of his tongue. When he finally pulled back, eyes glazed and lips wet, he looked both wrecked and impossibly hard.

I glanced down, and a flash of worry spiked through me. His cock stood at full, almost painful attention, the head flushed deep red and glistening with precum that dripped in steady, needy drops. It wasn't just a trickle—it was a testament to how far gone he was, how desperately he needed this.

"Strip," I commanded, voice dropping an octave. He obeyed, slipping out of the last of his clothes until he stood before me, naked and trembling. I spread my legs and pulled him down, the air around us crackling with urgency. The moment he positioned himself at my entrance, he thrust inside, a sharp cry escaping him as he sheathed himself in one swift motion.

It was frantic, an almost brutal joining that left me gasping, each thrust deeper and more desperate than the last. He didn't last long, barely a minute, his body shaking as he lost control. I felt the warmth spread inside me, and he groaned, the sound heavy with frustration and release. I tightened around him, riding out his shudders, a teasing smile on my lips as he met my eyes.

"You couldn't hold out, could you?" I whispered, taunting. But before I could say more, he was moving again, his cock still hard, sliding in and out with renewed intensity. This time, he set a punishing rhythm, each thrust rougher, more demanding. His fingers dug into my hips, pulling me against him, the sounds of our bodies slapping together filling the room.

"Do you want his cock?" he asked, voice rough and dark, a challenge and a plea wrapped into one. "Do you want to be fucked by his big, black cock?"

"Yes," I gasped, the brutal honesty of it leaving him stunned for a moment. "It's bigger than yours. You know it is."

He growled, a sound I had never heard from him before, and the pace increased, each thrust deep and hard, pushing me closer to the edge. "Do you want him to fill you up? To make you his?"

I moaned, arching beneath him, the words pushing me over. "Yes, yes, I want it. I want to be taken like that."

The admission sent him spiraling, his hands tightening on me as he slammed into me harder, the raw, animalistic need taking over. My body tensed, pleasure coiling tight and then breaking apart in a wave that left me shuddering and breathless. I cried out, the sound ripped from my throat as the orgasm consumed me, muscles clenching around him as I shook beneath him.

Seconds later, he followed, hips stuttering as he found his release, a strangled cry escaping him as he filled me again, warmth spreading between us. His body collapsed against mine, chest heaving, both of us slick with sweat and spent. The room was silent except for the sound of our breathing, the echoes of what we had just done hanging in the air.

WHAT NEXT?

In the months that followed, the memory of that night became a silent, powerful presence in our relationship. It was an unspoken bond that simmered beneath the surface, adding a charged edge to our intimacy. Sometimes, late at night, I would lean over to him, pressing my lips to his ear, whispering fragments of what I had done, letting the memory trickle back between us. I'd tell him how it felt, how he looked as he watched, the thrill that raced through me. His eyes would darken with that same mix of pain and desire, and before I knew it, we'd be caught up in the fever of it all, mouths and bodies entwined with an intensity that was almost frantic.

When I gave him head, the weight of what we weren't saying hovered between us. I'd catch his eyes as I moved, a flicker of acknowledgment passing silently from me to him—this was what turned us both on, what kept that fire raging. The heat in his gaze said it all, his fingers gripping my hair just a little tighter, hips moving a little more urgently. But even then, with our bodies sated and hearts racing, we never spoke of what came next. We danced around it, flirted with the edges of the memory, but we didn't dare name it aloud. It was as if putting it into words would unleash something too dangerous, too consuming, and we weren't ready for where that might lead.

stood in front of the mirror, adjusting the sleek, black leather dress that hugged my curves like a second skin. The material gleamed under the soft light, accentuating every dip and line of my body. The neckline plunged just enough to tease, exposing the tops of my breasts that pressed tantalizingly against the smooth fabric. The memory of our last encounter with Christian was still vivid, simmering in the back of my mind as I contemplated what tonight would bring.

Tonight was our anniversary, and I knew my husband had planned something special, the diamond bracelet I'd been pining for hidden in his pocket or wrapped carefully somewhere, waiting to be revealed. But I wanted to give him something that would leave a deeper mark, something that would make this night unforgettable. The decision had been building for weeks, ever since that night when I realized just how far we were both willing to go for that intoxicating mix of jealousy, power, and desire.

Christian had been receptive when I'd called, his voice carrying that unmistakable, playful edge. He had even suggested a few ideas that piqued my interest, ones that pushed just a bit further while staying within the boundaries that felt comfortable to me. The anticipation thrummed through me as I slipped on a pair of stiletto heels, the final touch that made me feel as powerful as I looked.

When I walked into the living room, my husband was already there, nursing a glass of whiskey, the anticipation in his eyes deepening when he saw me. He took in the dress, the heels, the deliberate sway of my hips as I approached, and I could see the realization dawn on him—tonight was going to be different.

"Happy anniversary, honey," I said, leaning down to press a slow, lingering kiss on his lips. His eyes searched mine, already dark with the promise of what was to come.

"Happy anniversary," he replied, voice thick as he set down his glass, unable to tear his gaze away from me.

I smiled and straightened, the room already buzzing with tension as I waited for the knock on the door that would change everything.

As my husband handed me the drink, I caught the glint of anticipation in his eyes. With a sly smile, I pressed my hand against his crotch, feeling the restrained throb beneath the fabric. "Well, you're going to have to wait a little longer," I whispered, letting my fingers curl and squeeze lightly. "Christian will be here soon."

A spark lit in his gaze, a mix of eagerness and torment. He swallowed hard and nodded, his Adam's apple bobbing. The minutes ticked by, heavy with anticipation, until the doorbell finally rang, slicing through the tension. My heart skipped a beat as I smoothed down my dress and opened the door to Christian's familiar grin. He was as tall and confident as I remembered, and as his eyes met mine, a surge of heat coiled low in my belly. I didn't know if the wetness pooling between my legs was from the sight of Christian himself or from knowing how wild it would drive my husband tonight.

I stepped forward and kissed Christian deeply, letting my body press flush against his, my breasts molding to his hard chest. The contact sent a shiver down my spine, and I let out a small moan as I reached between us and gave his cock a squeeze, feeling its girth stir beneath his jeans. "God, it's as big as ever," I said, loud enough for my husband to hear. I caught the way his eyes darkened, his breathing quickening as he stood a few feet away, watching.

As before, my husband climbed into the driver's seat, while Christian and I slid into the back. The hum of the engine barely covered the sound of my heartbeat as we pulled away from the house. Christian's hand found my thigh, squeezing possessively as he leaned in and claimed my mouth with a kiss that made my toes curl. I could feel my husband's eyes darting between us and the rearview mirror, the occasional quick glances telling me everything I needed to know. This was our dance—temptation and denial, pleasure and restraint.

Christian's hands roamed with newfound freedom, cupping my breasts and kneading them as our kisses grew hungrier. I could feel my nipples pebble beneath the tight fabric of my dress, a gasp slipping from my lips as his thumbs brushed over them. My husband's knuckles turned white as he gripped the steering wheel tighter, his breathing audibly heavy even from the front seat. If he could have, I knew he would have pulled over and lost himself in the moment.

As we drove further out, Christian gave my husband vague directions, keeping the destination a surprise. The dark highway stretched on, and the anticipation crackled in the air until we finally pulled into the lot of an erotic novelties store, isolated except for a closed coffee shop nearby. The thrill of being in such an exposed place made my husband's nervous excitement palpable. His eyes flitted around, checking for anyone who might see us, while Christian and I stepped out into the cool night air.

Inside, Christian and I stood close, our bodies brushing as if we were a couple. I reached for various pieces of lingerie, holding them up against my body and turning to Christian. "How about this one?" I asked, pouting playfully. He chuckled, eyes gleaming as he slid his hands over my waist. "Sexy, but I think you can do better," he replied, pulling a sheer, low-cut lace bodysuit from the rack.

The counter-girl raised an eyebrow as she watched me kiss Christian, our bodies pressed tightly together. "Who's paying?" she asked, a hint of curiosity in her voice.

I tilted my head and pointed to my husband, who stood a few feet back, shifting uncomfortably. "He will," I said, my tone light but dripping with the power I felt. The girl's eyes widened, a bemused smile tugging at her lips before she offered a knowing wink and rang up the purchase.

We piled back into the car, the ride electric with anticipation as we headed to a nightclub in the next town. The bass thumped through the floor as we walked in, the dim, pulsing lights casting shadows that danced over our skin. The moment we hit the dance floor, I turned to Christian, letting the beat guide my hips as they swayed in rhythm with his. The air between us was thick with heat, and when the music slowed, I pressed against him, feeling his body respond as we moved as one.

My husband watched from the bar, fingers drumming against his glass, eyes glued to me as I laughed and turned, grinding against Christian's hips. Each glance at my husband confirmed what I already knew—he was straining, wanting, unable to look away. When the song changed, I broke away, dancing with a group of other black men who were quick to join, their hands grazing my waist as I moved, pushing the edge just enough to keep my husband on the precipice.

By the time I returned to Christian, the look in my husband's eyes was pure, unadulterated lust. His cock, I was sure, could have punched through steel. The night was far from over, and we all knew it.

The living room was dimly lit, the soft glow of the lamp casting warm shadows over the room as Christian and I settled on the couch. My husband hovered nearby, a mixture of apprehension and anticipation etched on his face. His eyes darted between us, fingers clenching slightly as he watched me lean into Christian, our bodies close enough that my thigh pressed against his.

"Drinks," I said, tilting my head toward my husband. He snapped out of his trance, nodding quickly and heading to the kitchen. The clink of ice and the splash of liquid were the only sounds in the room as Christian's eyes met mine, dark and hungry. When my husband returned with the glasses, I took mine with a small smile, letting my fingers brush his just long enough for him to feel the heat in my touch. The music started, a slow, sultry beat that seemed to sync with the thud of my heart.

Christian turned to me, and before I could take another sip, his mouth found mine. It was deep and unhurried, the kind of kiss that claimed and teased all at once. Our tongues met, sliding together in a dance that made me forget for a moment that we weren't alone. My husband's presence lingered just at the edge of my awareness, the sound of his breathing reminding me that he was watching every second, riveted and helplessly captivated.

After what felt like an eternity, I pulled back, my lips tingling, and stood. "I'll be right back. Something cooler might be in order," I said, my voice light and teasing. Christian's smirk widened as he took a sip from his drink, leaning back comfortably as he watched me leave the room.

I changed quickly, slipping into the sheer lace bodysuit and the sky-high heels he'd picked out at the store. The lace hugged every curve, leaving little to the imagination, the delicate fabric stretching over my hips and clinging to my breasts. A sliver of doubt tickled at the back of my mind—I wasn't a teenager anymore, and this outfit revealed everything. But the second I stepped back into the room and Christian's eyes roved over me, followed by a low, appreciative whistle, the doubt melted away. My husband's mouth parted slightly, eyes darkening as he drank in the sight.

"Where were we?" I asked, letting my voice drop as I crossed the room and sat back down beside Christian. My hand found his thigh, squeezing lightly before sliding up to the hard ridge straining beneath his pants. His breath hitched, eyes gleaming with anticipation as I pressed my palm against him, feeling the heat through the fabric.

The room fell silent, save for the music and the sound of our breathing. I met my husband's gaze, a silent acknowledgment of the power I wielded in this moment, and then turned my attention back to Christian. My fingers found his belt, tugging it free with a deliberate slowness, the metal buckle clinking softly. One by one, I undid the snap and pulled down the zipper, the sound loud in the stillness.

My hands shook just enough for me to feel it as I reached inside and pulled out his cock. It was as big as I remembered, thick and pulsing with life. I let out a small gasp, the memory of the last time washing over me in a hot wave. I wrapped my fingers around him, feeling his weight and warmth, and leaned in just enough for my husband to see the smile that played on my lips.

"Honey, do you like what you see?" I said, glancing over my shoulder as my hands worked up and down Christian's cock, my touch firm and deliberate. The air crackled with tension, and I could see my husband's eyes widen, darkened with a mix of longing and disbelief. He sat transfixed, breath hitching as he watched, unable to look away.

Christian leaned back, his muscles tensing as he groaned, the weight and heat of him pulsing in my hands. I caught my husband's reaction in my periphery, his fingers twitching with the need to reach for himself, a battle raging inside him. The power I felt sent a thrill through me, but it came with a twist of something more complex—an edge of guilt that I couldn't ignore.

"Why don't you suck on it? Give your husband a real show," Christian said, his voice deep and confident. The request sent a shiver through me, but I shook my head, the boundaries I held onto surfacing despite the heat coursing through my veins.

Christian's eyes glinted as he took in my hesitation. "Then at least show me those beautiful tits," he suggested, voice smoother, coaxing. I hesitated only for a moment before tugging the top of my lace bodysuit down, letting my breasts spill out. My husband's sharp intake of breath was immediate, and he leaned forward in his chair, eyes locked on me with an intensity that made my skin flush.

Christian reached out, cupping my breasts in his strong hands, his thumbs brushing over my nipples, sending jolts of pleasure down my spine. I arched into his touch, my hands never leaving his cock as I continued to stroke him. My husband shifted, unable to stay still, and I could almost feel the war inside him. The sound of his breathing grew louder, more erratic.

"I want to suck on them," Christian murmured, eyes never leaving mine. I glanced at my husband, catching the barely restrained pleading in his expression. A moment passed, thick and heavy, before I nodded. Christian's mouth descended, warm and insistent, his tongue circling one nipple as he sucked and nipped. A moan slipped from my lips, unbidden, and my husband's reaction was visceral—a low, guttural noise that filled the room.

I kept pumping Christian's shaft, feeling the heat and slickness as he throbbed in my grip. My hands grew tired, but I didn't stop. The way Christian groaned into my chest only spurred me on. He pulled back slightly, catching my eye with a familiar, challenging look.

"Kiss it again," he said, the words a dare. I hesitated, glancing at my husband, who was gripping the arms of the chair, the conflict on his face plain as day. I could see the moment he broke—his hands reached down, pulling his cock free. It was hard, straining, but in that second, I felt a pang of guilt slice through me as my eyes flicked between him and Christian. The difference was stark, undeniable, and shame flared hot in my chest.

"Stop," I said sharply, forcing my gaze back to my husband. The guilt clung to me, but I pushed it down. "You know the deal. If you touch yourself, I stop this instant. Do you understand?" My husband's eyes met mine, raw with need and humiliation, and he reluctantly pulled his hand away, his cock twitching as he did.

"Good boy," I said, voice softening. "Had you kept going, I wouldn't do this…"

The room seemed to hold its breath as I leaned forward, pressing my lips to the head of Christian's cock, feeling the searing heat of him against my mouth. The taste was salty and intimate, sending a wave of reckless excitement through me. My husband's eyes were wide, jaw slack, as he watched. A mix of power and guilt twisted inside me, but the rush was undeniable.

I kissed it again, lingering longer, my lips parting to let my tongue flick against the tip. Christian groaned, a sound that made my toes curl. The moment stretched on as I opened my mouth wider, taking him in, inch by inch, until my lips stretched tight around his girth. The realization of what I was doing, here, in front of my husband of more than twenty years, sent my head spinning.

Christian's hand slid into my hair, guiding me as I moved, taking him deeper, each motion deliberate. My husband's eyes were locked on the scene, his own arousal unchecked but hands now obediently still. The power I felt was dizzying, leaving me breathless and hungry for more.

Out of the corner of my eye, I caught my reflection in the mirror above the mantel, and the sight made my breath hitch. There I was, draped in the sheer lace bodysuit, my breasts spilling out, nipples taut, hair disheveled and eyes wild. I looked like a woman I barely recognized, one who had shed inhibition and embraced the reckless, thrilling power of this moment. My lips wrapped around Christian's thick, veined cock, glistening with my own saliva. The image was both shocking and intoxicating, a stark contrast to the composed, devoted wife I had been for over two decades.

FROZEN

My husband sat frozen, eyes wide and dark, his mouth slightly open as if words failed him. The look on his face was a mixture of disbelief, awe, and longing. The rush of control that surged through me at that moment was unlike anything I'd ever felt. I pulled Christian's cock from my mouth, running my tongue along its length, tracing the prominent veins as I held it against my face. The weight and heat of it were undeniable, and when I pressed it so that his balls rested against my chin and the tip nearly touched my forehead, the thrill deepened.

Christian's smirk turned wicked as I tilted my head, letting him lightly slap my face with his cock. The sound was a soft, teasing thud that made my husband's breath catch audibly.

"Like what you see, dear?" I asked, my voice dripping with playful cruelty. "Does it turn you on to see me sucking this fat black cock with the lips I kiss you with?" I didn't wait for his response; the answer was written in the way his fingers twitched on the armrests, his chest heaving.

I dropped to my knees, the plush carpet digging into my skin as I took Christian's cock back into my mouth. This time, there was no hesitation. I moved slowly at first, savoring the feel of him as he pushed against my tongue, deeper with each pass. His taste filled my senses, an intoxicating mix of musk and salt, and I found myself lost in the rhythm. I felt his hand rest on the back of my head, a gentle pressure guiding me as I sucked him, my lips stretched tight and wet around his girth.

I withdrew for a moment, catching my breath as I let his cock slide against my breasts, dragging it across my nipples, which were slick and sensitive. Christian groaned, the sound vibrating through his body and into mine. The sight of my husband watching, eyes wide and tortured, sent a thrill down my spine. I spit lightly down the length of Christian's shaft, using my hands to coat him with the slickness, my palms sliding smoothly as I pressed my breasts together and trapped him between them. The friction was exquisite, and each time I pushed my breasts up and down, his cock throbbed, leaking precum that shone in the dim light.

The taste lingered on my tongue, a bitter reminder of what I usually detested. But tonight was different. Tonight, I was so turned on, so desperate to push this moment further, to please Christian and make my husband witness what I would never do for him. The raw need propelled me forward, past my aversion and into a place where the thrill outweighed the discomfort.

I felt Christian's shaft pulse under my touch, the tension in his body coiling tighter as he approached the edge. My mind screamed at me to pull away, to keep this moment from crossing into the irreversible, but something inside me, a raw and defiant part, refused to stop.

Without thinking, I took him back into my mouth just as he reached the point of no return. The first spurt of his cum hit my tongue, hot and more bitter than I remembered. The taste made me shudder, the urge to pull away surging up, but I pushed it down. I wanted my husband to see this, to know that I was doing this—something I never did for him—because I was caught up in the power and heat of it all.

Christian's hand tightened in my hair as he groaned deeply, his body jerking as he released into my mouth. I swallowed, fighting back the grimace that threatened to show, each gulp pushing me past my discomfort and deeper into the forbidden. The warm, salty taste lingered unpleasantly, but I kept going, sucking him as he moaned his appreciation, my heart thundering in my chest.

My husband's eyes were glued to the scene, his expression one of stunned arousal, unable to comprehend what he was witnessing. The power coursing through me was overwhelming, blurring the line between pleasure and taboo.

Christian's breathing grew ragged, and I felt his body relax as the last of his release spilled from him. I swallowed one final time, the taste making my stomach clench, but the rush was undeniable. I pulled back, my lips tingling, and met my husband's wide eyes. There was a spark in the air, something raw and unspoken that charged the space between us.

For the first time, I had swallowed another man's cum, something I had always sworn against. The realization was heady, powerful, and changed everything.

After I cleaned up in the bathroom, smoothing my hair back and catching my breath, I returned to the living room where Christian waited. I crossed the room and gave him a deep kiss, tasting the remnants of everything we had shared. He pulled back, eyes searching mine with a knowing, satisfied glint. My husband sat nearby, eyes unfocused, looking as though he were on the verge of passing out from the sensory overload.

But Christian wasn't quite done. With a mischievous smirk, he reached down, his hand sliding between my legs to press against my pussy through the thin lace of my bodysuit. I gasped, my initial reaction to clamp my thighs shut, trapping his hand there. The defiance was instinctive, a final grasp at control, but when his fingers pressed insistently, finding the heat and wetness seeping through the fabric, I couldn't fight the desire that flared to life. My legs relaxed, opening for him as my breath came in shallow, uneven pants.

"Can I open this?" he asked, his fingers playing with the edge of the fabric at my crotch, hinting at what lay beneath. I met his eyes, the pulse in my neck racing, but I shook my head, voice low and raw. "Not yet."

He didn't push further, but he didn't stop either. His fingers rubbed slow, deliberate circles over the sensitive spot, pressing just enough to make my thighs quiver. My back arched, and a soft moan slipped from my lips as the pressure built, heat pooling deep inside me. My husband's eyes widened, dark and hungry, as he watched, helpless to move but unable to tear his gaze away.

The sensation climbed higher, every nerve in my body focused on the friction of Christian's touch. The lace was soaked, clinging to me as I rocked against his fingers, my breaths turning ragged. When the wave finally crashed over me, I trembled, hips jerking as I came, the fabric beneath his fingers wet with my release. Christian's mouth found mine again, and we kissed with the lingering taste of my climax hanging between us, sealing the moment.

With a satisfied grin, he pulled back and stood, casting a glance at my husband, who sat on the edge of his seat, trembling with need. Christian nodded, a silent farewell that carried a weight of its own, before he turned and left, leaving the room filled with the scent of arousal and the echoes of everything we had done.

The minute the door clicked shut behind Christian, my husband practically lunged at me, hands shaking as they reached for my waist, eyes glazed with an almost feral need. I pressed a firm hand against his chest, stopping him in his tracks and guiding him back onto the couch. His chest rose and fell in quick, shallow breaths as I knelt between his legs, meeting his gaze with a knowing look that made his anticipation spike.

My fingers wrapped around his cock, already rock-hard and dripping with precum, a testament to how wound up he was from watching everything unfold. The contrast between him and Christian was stark, the memory of Christian's size and endurance still fresh in my mind. I couldn't help the fleeting thought that flickered as I looked at my husband—how he seemed so small in comparison, both in presence and performance.

I leaned forward, taking him into my mouth with practiced ease. His hands buried themselves in my hair, but his control was already slipping, his hips jerking up to meet my mouth as if he couldn't help himself. I worked him with precision, my tongue swirling around the head before sliding down the length, taking him deep and letting the warm, wet friction drive him mad.

It only took seconds for the tension to gather in his body, his thighs quivering under my hands. I heard him let out a strangled moan, and before I could even quicken my pace, his breath caught, body going rigid as he came. The rush of his release hit the back of my throat, warm and fast, and I swallowed automatically, the taste familiar and yet somehow unsatisfying after what I had just experienced with Christian.

As he slumped back, chest heaving and eyes shut tight, the realization hit me, and a wry smile tugged at my lips. I couldn't hold back the words that slipped out, laced with teasing and something sharper, something cruel. "Not only is his cock so much bigger," I said softly, my voice barely above a whisper, "but at least he doesn't cum in 30 seconds."

My husband's eyes flew open, the flush on his cheeks deepening as the humiliation set in. His mouth opened as if to speak, but no words came out, just a strangled sound that hung in the air. The weight of my statement settled between us, a reminder of the boundaries we had pushed, and how far we had fallen past them.

I reclined on the couch, letting the plush cushions cradle my back as I watched my husband's expression—flushed, eyes wide with a mix of humiliation and desperate arousal. The tension crackled in the room, thick enough to taste. I let my hand trail lazily over my thighs, teasing the hem of the lace bodysuit still clinging to my body, the damp spot at the center hinting at how far we had already gone. A sly smile played at my lips as I leaned back, spreading my legs slightly.

"I guess I don't need to ask if you like watching me suck on that big black cock, do I?" I said, tilting my head and catching the flicker of shame and hunger in his eyes. He swallowed hard, unable to respond, his gaze fixed on me like I was the only thing anchoring him to reality.

"Now get on your knees and lick my pussy."

He hesitated only for a moment before sinking down, his lips parting as he pressed his mouth to me, tongue sliding over the lace barrier still covering me. The fabric grew wetter as he worked, the heat of his breath seeping through, making my body respond despite the cold edge of control I wielded over him. I arched my back, a moan escaping my throat as he licked with the urgency of a man who knew he was both indulging and atoning.

But I wasn't going to let him forget. "His cock was so big, I almost couldn't fit it in my mouth," I said, my voice a teasing purr. I felt his movements falter for a split second, the sting of my words sinking in before he resumed, more fervent than before. "But I did it. And do you know how I felt, on my knees, with his fat cock filling my mouth?" I paused, savoring the tremor that ran through him. "I felt like such a slut. A willing, eager slut."

My husband's tongue pushed deeper, his breathing growing ragged against my skin. I threaded my fingers into his hair, pulling him closer, relishing the contrast between his desperation and the control I held. "I wonder how it would feel if I took it into my pussy," I mused, the idea rolling off my tongue as though it were idle conversation. His shoulders tensed, and I could hear the strangled sound he made, halfway between a moan and a plea.

"But you wouldn't want that, would you?" I continued, letting my voice drip with mock innocence. "For me to be fucked by that big, black dick. For me to know how it feels to be stretched by something that thick, to have my pussy wrapped around it, begging for more. No," I whispered, my nails scratching lightly at his scalp. "You wouldn't want that. You're scared I'd get addicted. Because, after all, his cock is so much bigger and better than yours."

His movements quickened, and I felt the shudder in his body as my words tore through him. He was driven by an unspoken need, each lick a silent submission, a plea for forgiveness or maybe for more.

I reached down and guided him up, pulling him over me. He climbed on top, his cock already hard again, throbbing as he pressed it against me. I allowed him to enter me, letting out a gasp as he pushed inside, his breath hitching as he filled me with frantic, jerky thrusts.

I let him set a rhythm, but I didn't let the tension drop. "But what if I get too excited?" I whispered, my voice wicked and taunting in his ear. His pace stuttered, the words slicing through him like a blade. "What if I forget to take my pills? What if I forget to tell him to wear a condom? What then?" His eyes met mine, wide and stricken, his face flushed as he fought to maintain control. "You wouldn't want that, would you? You wouldn't want me to get knocked up by a black man. For everyone to see my belly, big and fat with another man's baby, all because you wanted this, because you needed to see me like this."

His moans turned ragged, his hips slamming into me with abandon. I felt the shiver that ran through him, the telltale sign of his climax building. "What would the neighbors say?" I teased, my voice a breathless mockery. "Seeing me walking around, heavy with his baby? Knowing that I'm owned, claimed by him?"

That was all it took. His eyes squeezed shut, and a strangled cry broke from his lips as he came, hips shuddering against mine as he spilled inside me. The tension snapped, leaving him trembling and spent, his body collapsing onto mine as he struggled to catch his breath.

I lay beneath him, the room spinning with the aftermath, a small, wicked smile tugging at my lips. I had him, and we both knew it. The line had been crossed, the power exchanged, and there was no going back.

After that night, everything shifted between us. We didn't see Christian for a while, as if we both needed time to process the line we had crossed. The memory of him, the forbidden touch and taste, lingered in the air like an electric charge, sparking between my husband and me in the most unexpected moments. Our sex life was revitalized in ways I could never have imagined. Each time we were together, it was as if that night replayed in his mind, fueling a hunger that had been buried for years. The way he looked at me, touched me, spoke to me—it all carried the weight of that night's intensity.

Despite the passion that now flared so readily between us, I couldn't help but reflect on what I had done. The sheer audacity of it, the way I had taken control, was as thrilling as it was unsettling. It felt like a different part of me had been unleashed, a part that I wasn't sure I could tuck away again. The moments when my husband would close his eyes, still breathless and sated, I would lie awake, replaying the scene in my head, the image of Christian's dark eyes, the way he'd taken me to that edge.

With my husband's forty-first birthday approaching, I found myself thinking about how to capture that same fervor, how to give him something that would make his pulse race. Ideas spun in my mind, each one walking the tightrope between excitement and hesitation. I wanted to give him more, to push that boundary just enough to ignite us without crossing the line I wasn't ready to breach.

I still clung to my marriage vows, the promise that had bound us for years. They meant too much to me to risk shattering them completely. But every so often, when I thought of Christian or felt that tug of temptation, I could feel my resolve waver, just for a moment. The pull was there, subtle but persistent, reminding me that the edge we had danced along was still within reach, waiting, daring me to see how close I might come to it again.

FINAL ACT

Now, before you think I just spread my legs for him, I want to tell you that you're wrong. The first time I gave him a hand job, and the second time, I blew him. But that was it. My marriage vows were important to me, a line that defined my loyalty and my sense of self. As for being fucked, well, I had always believed that my pussy belonged only to me and my husband. The idea of crossing that boundary had always felt too far, a bridge I couldn't imagine burning.

Sometimes, in the quiet moments, I would feel a pang of guilt about what I had done. The thought of my husband watching me with Christian, seeing me in such a raw, unfiltered state, would make me flush with both embarrassment and something darker. But that feeling never lasted long. As soon as Christian left, my husband would be all over me, filled with a renewed hunger that burned away the shame. For weeks after, he would fuck me like a man possessed, driven by the memory of what we'd shared, and I'd find myself equally ignited, thrilled by how naughty and defiant it all felt.

I found myself toying with the idea of doing something even more daring for the next time—being totally naked or using a dildo while I jerked Christian off, pushing the edge just a little more. I called him to arrange a night, setting it up in a way that would thrill my husband without crossing the final line I swore to hold.

But life, as it often does, got in the way. The week turned into a chaotic whirlwind of work and responsibilities, and the plans I'd made slipped my mind.

When I finally walked into the house that evening, a full two hours late, the sight that greeted me made my breath catch. There, sitting comfortably in the living room with a relaxed, amused smile, was Christian. My husband stood nearby, hands in his pockets, shifting from foot to foot with a mixture of excitement and nervous energy. I flushed, embarrassment prickling over my skin as I took in my appearance—still clad in my somewhat frumpy work outfit, a far cry from the sultry, carefully chosen clothes I usually wore around him. My hair was pinned up messily, and the long day was etched in the slight smudge of my makeup.

Christian laughed, the sound low and warm. "It's okay," he said, eyes gleaming as he looked me up and down. The casual acceptance in his tone eased the tension a bit, and I felt a small smile tug at my lips, the embarrassment ebbing just enough for my pulse to quicken.

We settled in, beers in hand as the atmosphere shifted, tension turning from awkward to charged. My husband, ever eager to set the right tone, put on some soft, rhythmic music that thumped quietly in the background, mingling with the low buzz of conversation. The three of us spoke easily, but there was an undercurrent that hummed beneath the surface, anticipation twisting with each stolen glance and brush of a hand.

Christian moved closer, sliding next to me on the couch, the leather warming under our combined heat. His fingers brushed my arm, and when I looked up, he caught my gaze, leaning in for a kiss. It started light, a gentle press of lips that hinted at what lay beneath. But then it deepened, his mouth parting, tongue sliding against mine in a way that made my body tense and my breath hitch. The day's fatigue melted away, replaced by the familiar, electrifying rush that only came when Christian was near.

"Were you upset that I kept you waiting?" I asked softly, my voice breathless as I pulled back just enough to meet his eyes.

His hand slid down to rest on my thigh, fingers flexing possessively. "Not at all," he murmured, a smile curving his lips. "You're worth waiting for."

The words sent a jolt straight to my core, a flush rising to my cheeks as I felt my body react, heat pooling low in my belly. I glanced at my husband, who sat across from us, eyes dark and focused, watching with an intensity that mirrored the last time Christian had been in this room. The tension hung thick, poised on the edge of what we might do next, and I knew that tonight, just like before, we were about to push the boundaries a little further.

My husband's eyes were wide, pupils blown with desire as he watched from his seat. He was even more turned on than usual, and I could see it in the flush that crept up his neck, the way his chest rose and fell as if he were struggling to catch his breath. Later, he would tell me it was the sight of me still in my prim work clothes, disheveled and kissing Christian with abandon, that had driven him wild.

Christian's hands were confident as they cupped and played with my breasts, fingers squeezing and exploring with a boldness that grew each second. The fabric of my suit jacket bunched under his touch before he slid it off my shoulders, handing it to my husband without so much as a word. My husband took it, moving as if in a trance, and hung it up, eyes darting back to us as if he couldn't bear to look away for more than a moment.

Christian's fingers moved with deliberate slowness, undoing each button of my stiff, conservative white cotton blouse. The anticipation pooled low in my belly, spreading warmth that made my legs press together instinctively. He tugged the blouse open, revealing my plain white bra, a stark contrast to the way his touch made me feel. With a practiced ease, he unclasped the bra, letting it slide down my arms until it fell away.

I met Christian's eyes, a flicker of defiance sparking as I lifted one breast up to his mouth. He took it eagerly, tongue swirling over the nipple as he sucked, drawing a soft moan from me. My other hand reached for the untouched breast, and I leaned forward to tease the nipple with my own mouth, the sight of it making my husband's breath hitch audibly.

The weight of the moment pressed down on us, heavy and thrilling. I reached down, fingers trembling slightly as I freed Christian's cock from his pants. The familiar heft and heat of it filled my palm, the sheer size never failing to send a shock of awe through me. I stroked him slowly, eyes flicking between his face and my husband's, who was on the edge of his seat, eyes glassy with need.

"I'm sorry for being so late," I whispered, my voice low and filled with meaning as I worked Christian's shaft, feeling it throb in response.

Christian's smirk widened, a glint of mischief in his eyes. "Well, if you really want to show you're sorry, let me finger that pussy of yours," he said, voice deep and rough. A part of me hesitated, the boundary of what was allowed teetering on the edge, but when I met my husband's eyes, there was no doubt. He gave a subtle nod, the silent agreement that pushed me over that line.

My husband stood, guiding me up and reaching for the zipper on my skirt. The fabric slipped down my hips and pooled at my feet, leaving me in just my stockings and panties, the sheer material doing little to hide the wetness that soaked through. Christian's fingers were warm as they traced over my thighs, teasing at the edge of the fabric before slipping under. The first touch of his fingers against my slick heat made my breath catch, the electric sensation racing up my spine.

I gasped as he slid a finger inside me, the realization slamming into me—this was the first time anyone other than my husband had ever been inside me. The thought should have stopped me, but instead, it sent a shiver of excitement coursing through me, making my knees weak. The pressure and movement of his finger, slow and deliberate, coaxed a whimper from my lips. "Oh fuck," I whispered, unable to contain it, the words spilling out as heat coiled tighter in my core.

Christian's grin was feral as he fingered me, his hand moving with a confidence that matched the gleam in his eyes. My husband's gaze was locked on us, the tension in his body palpable as I stroked Christian's cock with one hand, the other bracing against the arm of the couch to steady myself. The combination of sensations, the unfamiliar touch inside me, and the way my husband's eyes devoured me, sent me over the edge. My body clenched around Christian's fingers, the climax crashing over me and leaving me breathless, thighs trembling as I gasped for air.

"Now," Christian said, voice dark and commanding as he leaned in, "what we should do is go over to that bedroom and let me stick my cock into you. And don't tell me that 'respect my marriage' shit, because your husband is all for it." His gaze flicked to my husband, who nodded, an eager, almost pleading look in his eyes.

The room spun, reality blurring with desire as I stood there, caught between the weight of my vows and the pull of something I could no longer deny.

I couldn't take it anymore. The tension was suffocating, the heat building until it was unbearable. One last shred of my conscience fought to hold on, giving me an out I could cling to. "Only if you have condoms," I said, my voice shaking with both anticipation and trepidation. Christian's smile widened, a knowing, triumphant glint in his eyes as he reached into his pocket and pulled out a box—a full twelve-pack.

I glanced at my husband, waiting for him to tell me no, to pull me back from the brink. But instead, he met my gaze with a look that was desperate and encouraging, a silent permission that sent a shiver down my spine. My resolve crumbled, and any barrier left between us dissolved in that moment.

The three of us made our way to the bedroom, the room where my husband and I had shared countless intimate moments. It felt surreal, the familiar space now tinged with an electric, forbidden anticipation. I felt my heart pounding as Christian's hand found my waist, pulling me close as we made out on the very bed where my husband and I had slept, laughed, and loved. His lips moved over mine, commanding and confident, and I felt myself yield completely, the last trace of restraint slipping away.

"Are you sure you want this?" I said, breaking the kiss to look over at my husband. My chest tightened with the gravity of what we were about to do. "There's no going back after this."

His eyes shone with a mixture of excitement and fear, and he nodded, the motion both resolute and trembling. "I'm sure," he said, voice thick and barely above a whisper.

I took a shaky breath and gestured for him to remove the rest of my clothes. His hands were gentle but trembling as he slid my panties down my legs, leaving me clad only in the stockings that hugged my thighs. Christian watched, eyes dark and focused, his chest rising and falling steadily as he absorbed the scene. When I was fully exposed, I nodded at my husband, and he stepped back, the anticipation on his face making my pulse race.

Christian reached for the box and tore it open, sliding one of the condoms out and rolling it down the length of his thick, dark cock. Even stretched to its limit, the latex barely seemed to fit, and the sight sent a thrill of disbelief coursing through me. The room was silent except for the rustle of the sheets as I moved to the center of the bed, positioning myself on my back with my legs spread, the cool air making me shiver.

Christian climbed onto the bed, his weight shifting the mattress beneath us. His eyes met mine, searching for any sign of hesitation, but I only nodded, unable to trust my voice. He leaned down, positioning himself, and I felt the tip of his cock press against me, warm and insistent. The pressure made my breath hitch, every nerve in my body poised on the edge of something I couldn't yet comprehend.

I turned my head, catching my husband's eye one last time, my voice trembling. "There really is no going back."

His response was instant, a mixture of awe and raw need. "I know," he said, his voice cracking. "That's what I want."

The reality of the moment hit me like a wave. Here I was, with my legs spread wide, about to take a huge, black cock into my married pussy while my husband stood by, urging me on. It felt impossible, surreal, and yet, it was happening. Christian pushed forward, the tip parting me, and I gasped as he began to fill me, stretching me in a way I had never felt before. The heat, the pressure, the forbidden rush—it consumed me, and I knew in that moment, nothing would ever be the same again.

I had used dildos in the past that were close to Christian's size, but nothing compared to the feeling of the real thing. The warmth, the pulse, the sheer presence of him as he pushed inside me—it was overwhelming. The head of his cock slid in first, stretching me open with a delicious, slow pressure, followed by the thickness of his shaft that made me gasp. It was more than just the physical sensation; it was the sense of being completely taken, completely owned by him in that moment. My husband seemed to fade into the background as Christian's powerful body pressed down on me, every muscle taut and commanding.

We kissed deeply, the kind of kiss that swallowed any lingering doubt and stoked the fire coursing through my veins. Each inch of him pushed deeper, filling me in a way I had never experienced before. My fingers gripped the sheets, nails digging into the fabric as he bent my legs up, folding them beneath his chest to drive himself even deeper. The angle made me arch my back, a cry tearing from my lips as he hit a spot that sent shockwaves of pleasure through me.

For a brief moment, a flicker of worry crossed my mind. *What if the rubber slips?* The thought sent a jolt of adrenaline through me, but instead of pulling me back, it pushed me forward, igniting something even hotter. The tension coiled tighter, making every thrust sharper, every sound he made more intoxicating.

Our mouths met again, tongues tangling as I screamed out, "I love black cock!" The words spilled out before I could think, raw and unfiltered, a confession that sent Christian's movements into a new, frenzied pace. My moans filled the room, a constant, breathless chorus as he humped me harder and deeper than I'd ever been before. The slick sounds of our bodies colliding mingled with my gasps, the pressure building inside me until it threatened to snap.

The climax hit me like a wave, washing over me with a force that made my entire body tense, toes curling as I shuddered beneath him. I barely registered Christian's deep, guttural groan as he pulled out, the warmth of him leaving me feeling achingly empty. He stripped off the condom, the latex stretched so tight it looked ready to burst, filled with the evidence of what we'd just shared.

Before I could catch my breath, he leaned forward and smeared the warm, sticky goo onto my chest, painting my skin with it. I met his eyes, a spark of mischief passing between us, and without a second thought, I rubbed it in, feeling the heat seep into my skin, a mark that would linger long after this moment ended.

About ten minutes later, after the heat of our first encounter had settled into a simmering haze, I found myself on my knees,

Christian's cock hard again in my mouth. The taste of him, mixed with the remnants of our earlier intensity, sent a thrill down my spine as I worked my tongue over every ridge and vein. He groaned, fingers tightening in my hair as he guided me, setting a steady, demanding rhythm. The sound of my husband's breathing, shallow and strained, drifted from where he sat, watching with wide, reverent eyes.

Christian's eyes met mine, dark and filled with an unspoken command. He slipped another condom on, and before I knew it, he was behind me, one large hand pressing between my shoulder blades to arch my back. The anticipation sent a shiver across my skin as he positioned himself, and then, with a powerful thrust, he was inside me again, deeper than before. I gasped, my hands bracing against the sheets as my body adjusted to the pressure and fullness.

Each thrust sent my breasts swinging forward and back, the sensation making me moan uncontrollably. The sound of skin meeting skin was sharp, punctuated by the rhythmic slap of his hips against my ass. When his hand came down in a sudden, stinging slap on my rear, I cried out, the sharp heat spreading across my skin. The act of him taking control, of him owning my body in that moment, made the pleasure coil tighter in my core.

From the corner of my eye, I saw my husband shift, his hand moving tentatively to his pants. This time, I didn't stop him. I met his gaze over my shoulder, the tension in his expression transforming into a look of shock as I spoke.

"Yeah, honey! Whack off as my pussy gets pounded by a beautiful black cock," I said, my voice breaking on a moan as Christian pushed deeper. "Rub that little white cock of yours, honey! I may never go back to white again." The words poured out, raw and unchecked, each syllable slicing through the air and landing with palpable weight. I felt my husband's body jolt, eyes widening as my taunts hit home.

The thrill of it—of speaking those words, of seeing the flush of humiliation and arousal spread over my husband's face—sent me spiraling. I came hard, my body clenching and shuddering as pleasure rolled over me in wave after wave. My cries filled the room, echoing off the walls as Christian groaned, thrusts turning erratic.

With a final grunt, Christian pulled out, the heat of him leaving me trembling. He ripped the condom off, and before I could turn, I felt the first hot splash of his cum hit my back, spreading in messy, sticky trails down my skin. The warmth of it made me shiver, grounding me in the moment as the realization of what we'd done settled around us.

I turned my head, catching my husband's eye as he sat there, stunned, his cock still in his hand, glistening. "Get a hot towel," I said, my voice rough but firm. "Wipe my back and clean my tits." He moved without hesitation, disappearing into the bathroom and returning moments later with a damp towel. The soft fabric dragged over my skin as he cleaned me, the act both reverent and submissive.

When he was done, I cupped my breasts, shoving them teasingly close to his face. "You see these?" I whispered, leaning in until he could feel my breath against his skin. "You can't touch them." His mouth opened, eyes pleading, but before he could lean in, I pulled back, turning to Christian.

With a grin, I pressed my chest against Christian's mouth, letting him suck on my nipples as my husband watched, the weight of the moment hanging heavy between us. The dynamic had shifted, and we all knew it.

I leaned back on the bed, my body still buzzing from everything we'd done. Christian stood off to the side, slipping on his clothes, a satisfied smirk playing at his lips. My husband hovered near the bed, eyes darting nervously between us. I reached for him, grabbing his wrist and guiding him to his knees at the edge of the mattress.

"Come here, honey," I said, my voice low and commanding. "Show me how grateful you are. Lick my pussy. Taste how I've been stretched and filled by him." The flush that crept up his neck was deep and visible, the ultimate humiliation mixed with the lingering excitement still simmering in his gaze.

He leaned in, breath trembling as his mouth met me, tongue tentative at first. "Good boy," I whispered, threading my fingers into his hair and pushing him closer. "Taste what a real man leaves behind." The degradation in my words made him pause for a moment before he resumed, tongue working more desperately, the shame clear in the quiver of his hands.

"Look at you," I continued, the bite of my tone making my own arousal stir again. "Licking my pussy like the submissive little husband you are. Do you know what it felt like to be taken by him? To be stretched until I could barely think?" His response was a muffled moan, tongue flicking and circling as he obeyed, the humiliation etched into every motion.

I felt the familiar, tightening heat build in my core, the roughness of his stubble grazing my thighs as he lapped at me. My body arched, fingers gripping his hair tighter as I let out a gasp, pleasure surging through me. I came with a shudder, my thighs trembling as my husband tried to keep up, his mouth soaked with a mixture of my release and the remnants of Christian's presence.

As the last waves of my orgasm subsided, I pushed him back slightly, chest heaving as I caught my breath. He sat up slowly, and that's when I noticed the change in his expression—an intense embarrassment that clouded his features. I glanced down, expecting to see him still hard and ready, but instead, his cock was completely soft, lying against his thigh like he'd lost his arousal completely.

Annoyance flared up inside me, the question forming on my lips as I narrowed my eyes. But then I noticed the glistening drip at the tip of his cock, and my gaze moved to the floor in front of him. A large, sticky pool of cum had gathered there, evidence of his release. He had cum without even touching himself, the sheer humiliation and excitement too much for him to handle.

A small, incredulous laugh slipped from my mouth as I took it all in. "You came," I said, voice laced with mock disbelief. "You came without even touching your pathetic little cock. Just from licking my pussy and watching me get fucked by a real man."

He looked down, face turning crimson, unable to meet my eyes. The shame rolled off him in waves, and for a moment, the room was silent except for the sound of our breathing and the faint rustle of the sheets. The power dynamic had shifted completely, and the realization left us both reeling.

BOOKS BY THIS AUTHOR

Ruined: The Impact Of Bbc On A White Wife

It was at that moment I knew the damage had been done. As my husband Steve climbed on top of me I had to actually think about it. For the first time in my life, I had to ask myself the question.

Was it in yet?

I hated myself for even thinking it. I know how rude it is. I know how disrespectful it is. Although I can't really make any excuses. There was only one person to blame for this, and it was Caleb and his big black cock that had stretched me out only an hour before.

No, the only person to blame for this was me. I chose to suck black cock, I chose to cheat on my husband. Although my friend Lauren can probably take a tiny bit of the blame, but that's another story entirely.

But however I try to explain it, one thing is for sure. After what Caleb did to me, now my pussy is ruined.

Sharing Sarah: A Husband's Bbc Fantasy Becomes Reality

Her eyes softened, and she reached for me, pulling me close. "What is it? You know you can tell me anything."

God, I wanted to. But the words stuck in my throat, tangled up in fear and uncertainty.

"I love you..." I stammered, my voice barely above a whisper. "But..."

"But...?" Her eyes widened, and I could feel her heart beating against mine, fast and steady, while mine felt like it might explode.

I swallowed hard, feeling the panic rise in my chest. My hands trembled as I wiped the sweat from my brow, trying to buy myself another moment. "I... I have a problem with myself, and I don't know how I can talk about it."
Without hesitation, she wrapped her arms around me, hugging me tightly, her breath warm against my neck. "Tell me, sweetie. Whatever it is, I'm here."

Her touch soothed me, but only for a second. This was it. There was no turning back now. "Alright... the problem with me is that... I have a fetish about something..." The words felt clumsy, foreign, like they didn't quite belong in the air between us.

I felt her body tense slightly, though she remained silent. It was as if she was holding her breath, waiting for me to continue. Hell, I think I was holding my breath too.

"...and that something is... about you." I dragged the words out, my voice shaky and unsure, like I was testing the waters before plunging in.

"Me?!" she interjected, her voice sharp with surprise.

I winced, unable to meet her gaze. "Please don't hate me, but... I'd like to see you with someone else."

For a moment, the world stood still. The silence that followed was deafening, stretching out longer than I could bear. I couldn't look at her. My eyes were glued to the floor, as if facing her would make this all too real.

Big Black Guest: Every Good Deed Deserves A Reward

Fate. That is the only word to describe what happened. Sure, my wife Danielle had to make her choices, I get that, and I certainly had to make mine.

But what set all this in motion was pure luck. My boss, Chris, needed somewhere to stay after a freak accident at his place, and if I'm honest, he was as much a friend as a boss, so our spare room was always going to be on offer.

But what wasn't meant to be on offer was my wife!

Printed in Dunstable, United Kingdom